Contents

The Wily Witch

ONCE upon a time there was an old witch who lived in a hollow tree. There was more room inside the tree than you might have thought. She had a room down below where she lived, and above it there was another room where she slept. And above that again was the smallest room, for the tree grew narrower as it went higher. This was the spare room, where people could come and stay.

The witch loved having guests. She sat all day in the lowest room, looking out of the window. As soon as a stranger passed who seemed to be lost, she tapped on the glass and beckoned with her crooked fore-finger.

"Good day, dear boy, you are lost," she said. Usually the stranger stopped and asked: "How can you tell?"

"I can see it from your shoes, for they are broken. I can see it from your cheeks, for they are hollow. I can see it from your lips, for they are dry, my child. And your eyes are dull with need of sleep."

The stranger naturally was amazed that the witch knew all this and thought to himself: "She must be a witch."

· The old witch, who had been waiting for this, said quickly: "Of course you think I am a witch!"

Many felt so awkward then, for she really did look like a witch, that they had nothing to say.

"I *am* a witch, am I not?" insisted the old woman. "I entice lost persons into my house and give them good food to eat. When they are too fat to fit into the topmost room I put them in the one below, and when they no longer fit in *there*, they come down to the lowest room, and into the oven they go!"

And because she spoke so frankly, and smiled as she spoke, the people thought she was joking and went merrily in. But it was no joke, and they never came out again. And no one in the country could do

3

anything about it, for, after all, the witch warned all her guests in advance.

The mayor in whose district the tree stood discussed it with the cleric in whose parish the tree grew, but neither of them could see a way out.

"If only she didn't tell them *herself*," said the mayor, "then I could forbid the whole thing. But she makes it all quite clear beforehand and the people go in willingly."

"Just so," agreed the clergyman. "That is the awful thing about it. Look here: I can understand her enticing strangers in to make them fat and then baking them in her oven. I don't approve, but I can put myself in her place, and we all have our faults. But the fact that she speaks the truth about it is too much for me."

They shook each other by the hand and went on their way. And the witch went on baking. Time and again people would see the white plume of smoke coming from her chimney and they shuddered. She was giving the town a bad name, too. It grew smaller and smaller and the hotels began to fail sadly, for there were those who believed the town had a witch and they stayed away, while others did not believe it and *they* stayed in the hollow tree. In both cases the hotels were empty.

"We shall have to hire a wizard," said the mayor at last. "This cannot go on. Does anyone know a wizard?"

Now, a wizard had been living in the town for years, giving no real cause for complaint, so the mayor had never heard of him. He cast spells entirely for pleasure. He had changed the climbing rose on his wall into a vine and he owned a monkey, although everyone knew that it had been a dog originally. What is more, purely for his personal enjoyment he had filled his garden with toadstools, each with a little bell attached to its underside, which rang when the sun went up.

"I must have him," said the mayor. "Bring him to me."

He had scarcely said the words when the wizard stood before him.

"I see that you know your trade," said the mayor happily, "and I suppose you also know why I have summoned you?"

"The witch in the hollow tree," replied the wizard instantly, for this was a mere trifle to him.

"Quite right. And what is to be done about her?" The wizard pondered.

"Our powers are more or less equal," he said at last. "We're like two sides of a penny. What do I get for coping with her?"

"Two pennies," replied the mayor, for he knew that the wizard could turn any coin into a gold piece.

"Agreed," said the wizard. "I shall change myself into a wanderer who has lost his way . . . and he might as well look a little foolish, too."

"You can have some clothes from the Corporation," said the mayor, "but I would leave your face just as it is if I were you."

"All right," agreed the wizard, and with a muffled bang he vanished in a cloud of smoke.

An hour later he was walking like someone lost, past the hollow tree. The witch began to quiver with expectation, for she had seldom seen anyone who looked so ready to be fooled. She didn't even feel it necessary to beckon with her crooked forefinger, but threw the window open at once and cried:

"How worn your shoes are, how dry your lips, how dull your tired eyes; now just you come straight in!"

In her haste she missed mentioning the hollow cheeks, for she was hungry and the wizard looked well-fed.

"You can go straight up into the second room," she said briskly. "And if you eat up everything I serve you, we'll turn on the oven next week."

The wizard smiled. "You're joking," he said. "You certainly must be making fun of me."

"They all say that!" cried the little woman gleefully. "And that's why I always have something to eat!"

"Come now," insisted the wizard, "this is just funny talk."

"That's what you *think*," replied the witch, "but that doesn't mean it is *so*."

The wizard stopped halfway up the stairs and said: "Ha, ha! I really can't help laughing." He played the part of a foolish stranger perfectly.

After winning the old crone's confidence in this way he went to bed. Next morning he got up very early. He slipped down to the breakfast table and scattered some black powder in the teapot.

"A cup of tea?" asked the witch, coming into the room.

"None for me today," answered the wizard cunningly, "but go on and have yours." For he wanted *her* to drink it.

"Then we'll drink coffee," said the little woman, throwing the tea out of the window. She went to the kitchen to grind the coffee and meanwhile the wizard put some of the powder in the milk jug.

"Milk and sugar?" asked the witch, coming in with the coffee.

"*Just* sugar," replied the wizard craftily.

"That's what I like to hear," said the witch. "I've done the same for years."

The wizard now realized that he was dealing with a real witch, and he became so cunning that he sometimes amazed himself. And he felt glad at heart, for in the town, where he had lived among good men, he had had nothing to do, and for years the ringing of the toadstools had bored him.

"Have a peppermint?" he asked suddenly, producing a little bag. The witch had not thought of that. Absent-mindedly she popped one in her mouth and next moment she had turned into a hen. The wizard went up to fetch a basket, but when he came down again the witch was sitting in her chair, herself again.

"I had such an odd dream," she said, "but I won't tell you about it. Here's an egg for you!" For she had laid it in his absence. The wizard did not want to awaken her suspicions, so he ate the egg, humming to himself. The next minute he had changed into a dove. He flew upstairs at once and sat on the edge of his bed.

"Keep calm," he warned himself, "and don't lose your head. This shape can't last long."

He was right, because when sorcerers cast spells on each other they don't last as long as with ordinary people. When he was himself again, he went downstairs and took a ring from his finger.

"Allow me," he said. "A little gift. Shall we bet on whether it fits?"

"I wouldn't think of taking it," said the witch. "Some trifle, perhaps, but *this* is too much."

"Put it on just to please me," urged the wizard.

"I wouldn't think of it," replied the witch. "Such a beautiful ring it is! And I had just planned a little present for *you*."

She slipped over to the chest and pulled out an old watch.

"You just hold it against your ear, and then press *this* knob. Then you will hear a little tune—and what happens next will surprise you a lot."

The wizard began to laugh shrilly. "I know better than that," said he.

"Just as you like," replied the little woman coolly. "My house is yours."

The witch and the wizard sat opposite each other all day, racking their brains to find something that would give one of them the upper hand. Once the wizard turned the witch into a rat, but she slipped out and came back in her own form after a short walk, as if nothing had happened. Another time the witch turned the wizard into an owl, but he flew out of the window and rang the door bell not long after, as if he had noticed nothing. In the evening the witch went to the oven to bake some bread. She took the ash from under the stove and the ash-pan was full of buttons which had not burned up.

"Ugh," said the wizard, "aren't you ashamed?"

The witch blushed for the first time in her life and it was quite becoming.

"I enjoy it so much," she said. "And what else have I in my life?"

The wizard had never thought of that, and he looked at her tenderly.

"Do you think it is fun to be scorned because you are wicked?" sniffed the witch. "You are always alone—and nobody likes you."

"That's true," said the wizard, for he hadn't enjoyed it either.

"To live in a hollow tree," the witch went on, the tears pouring down her cheeks, "and have nothing to do all day but lure good men inside! If only you knew how they bored me! Not a single insult or mean trick, not even a small kick under the table from them—just friendly words. You wouldn't believe how relieved I feel when I've eaten up one of those simpletons. But it's not long before another one arrives."

"Dear creature!" cried the wizard suddenly. "Why don't we get married? We have so much in common."

Now the witch was speechless, for she had never thought of that.

"We're two bad people," the wizard went on, "and we can still get a lot of misery out of each other. Do say yes!"

"Yes," said the witch.

They rubbed their noses together, for such creatures do not kiss. And a great peace fell on the town. The two sorcerers continued to live in the hollow tree, but from then on the witch shook her head whenever strangers asked for shelter. She had no more interest in them, for each night her husband flew through the air on a broomstick, catching owls and bats, which tasted much better than people. They had more bones and they were tougher, and that was just what she liked best. And the two were so fond of each other that by evening they were tired out with shouting insults, and simply boxed each other's ears in silence.

One day, when it was the witch's birthday, the wizard, from pure affection, gave her such a crack with the frying pan that she fell stone-dead on the floor. Then the wizard began to pine, and a week later, he too breathed his last. The hollow tree is still there. But no one lives in it now.

The Lady
of the
Lake

ON a Friday night, when the moon is full, take care, for the world is bewitched. If on such a night you come to a lake, you will see the Lady of the Lake. She rises silently to the surface; not a ripple disturbs the water. She says nothing, but looks at you with her ice-cold eyes Then with her white hand she beckons and into the water you go, whether you want to or not. No one can help you. The water closes over your head and no mortal man knows what happens after that.

Now, once upon a time there lived a king and a queen who had only one child. He was the prince, and the prince was very spoiled. When he was still in his cradle he was given a golden rattle. He ate from a golden plate and he drank from a golden mug. All his toys were of gold and as he grew older it became more and more difficult to give him anything that he did not already possess.

By the time he was to be eighteen he had everything he could wish for, and all in pure gold. But he must be given something for his birthday. The prince stood by the window as his uncles and aunts filed in. Each one had brought him a present, but they felt very awkward, for they knew that he would have it already. The prince unwrapped the paper and took one look. "I have one of those," he said each time, and flung the present out of the window. Down in the snowy street stood the poor children of that country. They gathered up the presents and hurried home, where such things could be put to good use.

A young girl was standing there, too. She loved the prince dearly. She did not dare to say so, for she was very poor, but she *was* very fond of him all the same. She picked up a golden fiddle the prince had tossed away, and slipped it into her apron. But she did not go home. She waited and watched in the falling snow. All the children had gone, because

9

they thought that there was nothing more to come, but the girl stayed on. It was already twilight when she caught a gold mug. She tucked it into her apron, but still she did not go home. She waited there in the darkness, gazing silently upwards. It was bitterly cold and she could see the prince standing by the window, while a bright fire flickered behind him. There! He had been given yet another present. He unwrapped the paper, yawning, and a moment later a golden dagger flew out of the window. The girl picked it up and tucked it silently into her apron. Only then did she turn and go slowly home.

At that very moment the prince looked out of the window and saw the girl walking away. A trail of red drops of blood lay behind her in the white snow, for she had cut herself on the sharp blade, although she did not know it. The prince leaned out of the window and called:

> "Ho, maiden, bid you stay!
> Did I harm you in some way?"

The girl turned swiftly and replied:

> "More than you know
> You cause me woe."

The prince quickly forgot her, for other visitors arrived and he hoped that at last he would receive something that he did not already possess. But he had everything already and he yawned so hugely that tears sprang into his eyes.

"How boring it is when you already have everything," he said irritably. "I really think I will go to bed now."

And he would have done so, too, had not an old woman arrived just before midnight. The old woman was called the Princess Bobbelink. Princess Bobbelink had a strange, deep voice and a long, pointed nose, which always had a drip hanging on the end of it. She lived in a distant palace, where she opened the door to no one, for no one ever came to see her.

"So, dear boy," she rumbled, "have you had many presents?"

"Yes," said the prince, "but I have thrown them all out of the window. Have you brought something that I do not possess already?"

"I believe I have," answered the old woman. "Here it is."

And she gave him a big black book, wrapped in cobwebs.

"Bah!" said the prince. "Is that all?" He had already started towards the window, to fling the book out with the rest.

"Not so fast!" warned the old woman. "This is a book of spells.

Think of the oddest things you like, and you will find them there."

This promise aroused the prince's curiosity. Without even a word of thanks, he hurried off to his bedroom and began to read. The old witch was right. The oddest things you could think of were to be found there. First there were spells to turn the whole dinner service into silver. The prince passed over them, for he had already seen this done years ago. Then there were five pages about turning all the cups and saucers into gold. The prince flipped over these pages too, for he had been given golden cups and saucers on his last birthday. Then came the spells for conjuring roast venison out of nothing, and producing from two half-burned matches a stuffed hare which would melt on your tongue. The prince passed over these too, because he had often eaten such things before. Then he read that diamonds could be found under toadstools when there was a rainbow in the sky, and how to change hailstones into pearls just by standing quite still and thinking of nothing else.

The prince read on and on, but no matter how many pages he turned, he could find nothing that he did not already know about or possess. And he was just about to pitch the book out of the window when he came to a page which was stuck down by its two outer corners. The old woman had written on it in large letters: "DANGER! DO NOT OPEN!" for well she knew that was just what the prince would do.

And so he did. The prince tore open the page and read the story of the Lady of the Lake. "Friday and full moon," said he. "I would dearly love to see that Lady, because seeing her is the only thing I have not already done."

He looked out and saw that the moon was full in the sky. Then he called his chamberlain and asked what day it was.

"Friday, your Highness," answered the man, "and tomorrow it will be Saturday."

The prince gave him a florin because he knew more than he had been asked. Then the prince put on his ermine cloak and went out. The snow had stopped; it was a cold, bright night and the stars stood still in the sky. The prince looked curiously about him. The whole world was white and all the paths were covered with snow. And because he did not know which way to go, he followed the trail of the crimson drops of blood leading to the house of the young girl who had been cut by the gold dagger. She was standing by the window of her room, with a lighted candle in her hand.

"Can I come and sleep in your warm bed?" asked the prince.

"I shall have to ask my father," answered the maiden, "and I dare not wake him."

"But I am so cold," said the prince.

"That is not reason enough," said the maiden. "You must also love me truly."

"All right," said the prince, "I love you."

The girl shook her head. "Saying so is not enough," she said again. "You will have to prove it, too."

"How can I do that?" asked the prince.

"You must give up your plan to go to the Lady of the Lake," said the girl. "And if you promise that, then I will open the door to you in one hour."

"All right," said the prince. "I promise." For he really did find the girl very charming. But he did not love her truly, for he had never been taught to love anyone.

"An hour is a long time," warned the girl. "Will your love be equal to it?"

"Oh, yes, indeed," answered the prince. "I will prove it to you."

"We shall see," said the girl, "but I do not believe it."

And she was right, for after a quarter of an hour the prince felt so cold, standing in the snow, that he could not bear it any longer.

"I am going home," he said to himself. "I cannot bear it any longer, and we will see what happens tomorrow."

He had thought he would find the way home quite easily, but he was wrong. More snow had fallen meanwhile, covering the crimson spots of blood, and there was no sign of them. Hour after hour the prince wandered through the white snow and he was truly sorry that he had not waited, but now it was too late. He shouted for his valet and his coachman and all his servants, but they were all safe in bed and deaf to everything. He even shouted the names of his father and mother and all the aunts and uncles he could think of, but they did not hear him either.

At last the prince grew so cold that he could scarcely walk. His hands were frozen and he felt sleep slowly overwhelming him. The prince knew that if he slept in the snow he would never wake again, and he forced his eyes wide open. Suddenly he saw a wide, glassy lake. The moon was reflected in the still water and in the very middle of the lake the head of a woman rose slowly to the surface. She looked at him with her cold eyes and stretched out her arms to him. The prince felt an irresistible power drawing him as he stepped into the ice-cold water. It almost stopped his breath, but he walked on, for he could not do anything else. The water was up to his hips. It rose to his chest and reached his lips. Then the woman threw her arms about him, and swift as an arrow she plunged with him into the depths.

In the morning the palace was in an uproar. The servant who always carried the prince's breakfast up on a golden tray had found the bed empty. He immediately rang the silver bell which hung above the bed, and when the king heard it he sounded the great golden bell which hangs in the tower and soon all the bells in the land began to ring, because the prince was missing.

The young girl heard them, but she said nothing. She tucked the golden fiddle, the mug and the dagger in her apron, said goodbye to her father and mother and went straight to the palace.

All the wisest men in the land were gathered there. They stood before the king's throne, taking turns in guessing where the prince might be. One thought he had been swallowed by a whale, another was sure that he was flying through the air on the back of a black swan, a third said that a magician had changed him into a willow tree. The king listened attentively, for he was anxious to know the answer. At last he saw the young girl standing there and asked her what she thought.

"The prince is with the Lady of the Lake," she said.

The wise men laughed, for they did not believe in the Lady of the Lake.

"Sire," said one of them, "that is nonsense. The Lady of the Lake does not exist. The prince has been changed into a bluetit and is sitting on a roof somewhere." That was his own idea.

"Right," said the king. "You can all go home. The maiden will stay here."

When he was alone with the girl he said: "Open out your apron."

The maiden opened out her apron, and the golden fiddle, the cup and the dagger clattered to the floor.

"Strange," said the king, "how did you come by those?"

"The prince threw them all out of the window," answered the girl. "And what is thrown out of the window belongs to everyone."

"That is true," said the king. "And what are you going to do now?"

"I am going to look for him," answered the girl, "and when I have found him I will bring him here."

"Do that," said the king, "and go with God."

The girl gathered up the fiddle, the cup and the dagger and went out. When it was evening she reached a wide, frozen lake. She took out her fiddle and began to play. A little crack appeared in the ice, but the girl played on. The crack grew wider and at last she could see the water. It was quite black and ran in a narrow channel to the middle of the lake.

Then she took her golden mug and began to scoop up the water. It was icy cold, but the maiden went on scooping bravely, until she saw a long passage sloping downwards into the lake. The cold there was so terrible that it pierced through bone and marrow, but she walked down all the same, until she came to a door made of a single block of ice, as smooth as glass. The girl hesitated. There were no bell, no knob and no lock, and she realized that she herself must find a way to open the door. She took the dagger from her apron and blew on it with her warm breath. Then she traced an arch in the ice until she had made a whole doorway. She placed her bare hands against the ice and pushed. The archway she had cut fell in and the girl stepped through. There sat the Lady of the Lake, her arms about the prince, staring fixedly at the maiden.

"What have you come for?" she asked.

The maiden shivered, for even the lady's voice was cold.

"I have come to fetch the prince."

The Lady of the Lake smiled.

"If you can unloose my arm," she answered, "then you may take him with you." Within the circle of her embrace, the prince seemed lifeless.

The girl laid her hand on the lady's arm, and the arm was colder than the coldest ice. Though her fingers froze at once on the marble skin, she did not let go, but grasped the arm firmly.

"I love him," she said.

"That is not enough," answered the Lady of the Lake. "You must prove it."

"How shall I do that?" asked the maiden.

"My arm is frozen," answered the Lady of the Lake, "and no power on earth can release the prince from its clasp. But if you can hold on for one hour my arm will thaw and I will lose my power. Poor child, that you surely cannot do."

"That I can," said the maiden, "for I love him."

The Lady of the Lake smiled again. "We shall see," she said, "but I do not believe it. An hour is a long time. No love is strong enough for that."

As the girl held her icy arm, the Lady of the Lake looked into her eyes, until the maiden felt that she could no longer endure the icy gaze. She turned her head away to look at the prince. He was deathly pale and his eyes were closed.

"Look at me," said the lady.

"No," answered the maiden, "I will look at him." And she did. As she looked, his eyelashes quivered and a little flush came into his marble cheeks.

"Look at me!" commanded the lady.

"No," said the girl again. "I shall look only at him, for only then can I bear the pain I feel."

She ached as the blood froze in her body, but she held on, for she could also see that the prince was slowly coming to life. He opened his eyes and looked round him in amazement. Then he saw the maiden. He could not speak, but he looked earnestly at her, as if to say: "Keep it up a little longer. I shall be free soon and we will go away together." The maiden wanted to answer but she could not, for her lips were frozen and not a sound came from her mouth.

At last the prince stood up and took the girl in his arms. He carried her back into the icy passage and walked through the snow and wind, straight to the palace. There he held the frozen maiden fast against his breast until the warmth of his heart restored her and she looked about.

"Where am I?" she asked in astonishment.

"You are in the king's palace," answered the king, "and here you will stay."

And it was as the king had said.

Now the prince put on his best clothes and knelt at the maiden's bedside.

"Will you marry me?" he asked.

She only nodded, for talking was not easy yet, but that was enough. And they were married and were very happy. The fiddle, the dagger and the golden mug were placed on a velvet cushion and whenever the prince and princess had visitors they told their story. And if people found it hard to believe, after all, they could prove it.

The Tale of the Huntsman

ONCE upon a time there was a huntsman who had a wife and three children. He loved his wife, although he was also a little bit afraid of her, for she had a sharp tongue. But most of all he loved his children. There were two boys and a girl. One of the boys had coal-black hair and he was called Blacktop. The other was so fair that his hair was almost white and he was called Whitecrown. The little girl's hair was neither black nor white. You might have called it brown, but for the brighter flecks in it, and so she was called Dapple. She was a strange child, but we are just going to hear about that.

One day the huntsman was walking through the wood. He had shot nothing all day and when it was evening dark clouds began to gather in the sky.

"There is a storm coming," thought the man. "I must go home."

Suddenly he saw a stag on the bank of a stream. The water reflected its dappled flanks and slender legs and made its branched antlers ripple like swaying plumes. The creature slowly turned its head and looked calmly at him. The huntsman trembled, for the deer's look troubled him. He lowered his gun and said: "Go, for I cannot kill you."

The creature bowed its head and turned to go. But as it went one of its antlers struck a bough and a fragment of horn broke off. The huntsman picked it up and blew on it. It gave a clear and lovely note. "I have gained something after all," he thought. But as he went on he regretted his decision.

"How can I tell my wife about this?" he said to himself. "She will reproach me bitterly."

Scarcely had he said this when a wild swan flew silently above his head on snow-white wings. The huntsman raised his shotgun and was about to shoot when the same thought stayed his hand.

"Lovely creature," he said, "fly on, for I cannot kill you."

The swan bent its shining crown and vanished above the tree tops. The huntsman picked up a white feather from the ground.

"When my wife hears of this," he thought, "she will scold me."

No sooner had he thought this when he saw a coal-black raven on a branch. The bird was carrying a silver spoon in its beak, for ravens are thieves. The huntsman, who was an honest man himself, raised his gun resolutely and took aim. But he did not fire. For once again he heard a voice within himself which said: "Why? Did not God make this creature, too?"

The bird bent its head and vanished. And the silver spoon fell to the ground. The huntsman picked it up and went home with a heavy heart. He was just in time, for the thunder was already rumbling as he went inside.

"What have you shot today?" asked his wife.

"Nothing," said the man, and he told her what had happened, for he could not lie.

"Stupid," she said, "to let two birds and a deer go free. Do you know that you have three children? What are they to live on?"

The man bowed his head, for he himself did not know what had come over him.

"Perhaps I was really thinking of them," he said at last, "for the three creatures wanted to live, too."

His wife shook her head, because she had never heard anything so silly before. And she began to laugh when the huntsman put the piece of horn, the feather and the silver spoon on the table.

"Is that what you are going to feed them on?" she asked scornfully. "It is lucky I still have the hare from yesterday."

And she went to the oven, while the three children sat down at the table. Dapple took the piece of horn and Blacktop the silver spoon, but Whitecrown chose the feather. He was the youngest of the three, so he liked that best. And just as he was looking at the white piece of down, the storm broke in earnest.

The thunder crashed above the house, a mighty wind blew open the door and snatched the feather from the child's hand. The boy jumped up and ran after it as it sailed out. But on the threshold he shrank back fearfully. A blinding light flashed in his eyes and the lightning struck past him at the chair which he had just left. The back broke and a round hole the size of a fist was burned through the seat.

But when the smoke had cleared, the parents missed the child who had chosen the horn, and their thankfulness was turned to dread. This child, Dapple, was the most precious of the three. She was a silent little girl who could neither speak nor hear. She usually sat shyly in a corner of the room, startled by the slightest thing. And now she had run out through the open door, straight into the great forest. Her father ran out and called her name, although he knew that she could not hear him. Further and further he ran, and at last he had to accept the fact that the little girl was lost. Many wild animals lived in the woods and the child could not hear them coming, nor even call for help.

But suddenly her father stopped. Far in the distance came a sound as if someone had blown a horn. He ran from tree to tree in the direction of the sound and then he saw the little girl. She was sitting on the ground, leaning against a tree, and blowing on the horn she had chosen. And when she saw her father she jumped into his arms and kissed him. But she said nothing, for she could not speak. And the father too was silent. He clasped the child to his heart and stroked her wet hair.

But when he returned home with the little girl in his arms, his thankfulness was once again turned to fear, for there was a stranger in the house. He had taken the huntsman's gun and was looking fiercely about him.

"I am being pursued," he said. "Some silver has been stolen and I am suspected of the theft. I am innocent. But the soldiers are at my heels."

Then they heard voices about the house and someone banged on the door.

"Open in the king's name! We are looking for a thief."

The man aimed the weapon at Blacktop, who was still clinging to the spoon.

"Listen," he said softly to the huntsman. "If you shout back that

I ran past the house, your child shall live. But the minute you open the door I will shoot him through the heart."

The terrified boy backed against the wall, pressing his hands flat against it—the spoon fell tinkling to the floor. The stranger stooped and picked it up.

"The letters on the handle," he said, "stand for the owner's name. How did you come by this?"

Just then the door flew open and the soldiers rushed in.

"I did not do it," said the man calmly. "Ask the father of this boy how the spoon came here and let me go free."

So the huntsman told them that the raven had stolen the spoon and he even knew the place in the wood where the birds built their nests. And there the king's men found the rest of the silver. It was hidden in three nests and the ravens had taken weeks to gather so much plunder. The man was allowed to go free, but he did not go. He returned to the huntsman's house and said to the boy:

"You saved my life. Ask what you will, for I am a rich man."

The boy answered: "I would like my father not to have to hunt any more. He never enjoyed it, but now that all these things have happened it would grieve him every time he had to shoot an animal."

"Well said!" replied the man. "Your wish shall be fulfilled."

He took a purse from his pocket and turned to the huntsman.

"There are a hundred gold pieces in here," he said. "Buy a farm with them, with fields and cattle. You will still have some money left over. And once a year, on the boy's birthday, I will come and see if there is anything you lack."

The huntsman bought the farm and lacked for nothing. He no longer had to kill, but saw life being born about him. And the stranger kept his word. Every year he came to see them and gave the boy a silver spoon because it was his birthday. After twelve years the boy had a dozen silver spoons and that meant he could marry. And he did so. He lived in prosperity and told his children how poor he had been once. But they were all born with a silver spoon, and did not believe a word of it.

Princess Steppie

IT was a long, long time ago—not as far back as when animals could talk, but before my grandmother was born—somewhere between the two came the reign of King Boruba. Have you heard of King Boruba? No? Then it's high time this story was written. For this is a dangerous century for the storyteller: How easily he might fall under a bus; how readily a passing car might forever end humanity's chance of ever hearing King Boruba's . . . but have you really never heard of King Boruba? How odd!

What is fame upon this earth? Had you asked in King Boruba's day: "Who is King Boruba?" all the street urchins would have laughed you to scorn at once. People would have had doubts about your head— had the opportunity still existed. For there was a standing custom among the policemen of those days of chopping the head off anyone who doubted King Boruba. It saved legal complications, and it relieved any remaining doubters of the desire to express their feelings.

No one was allowed to doubt King Boruba. If he thought the azalea the loveliest flower of all, then the azalea *was* the loveliest flower. If he thought the bells in St. Martin's belfry chimed more sweetly than those in the cathedral of St. John, then St. Martin's bells *were* sweeter. If you prized carnations above azaleas, or preferred St. John's peal to St. Martin's, your head was chopped off. And, after all, we do have a preference for our own heads. People felt just the same in those far-off days; they kept quiet and said the king was a man of principle. You know what principles are, don't you? They come into the conversation at least once a day and it's not nice at all. "Excuse me, sir," says the otherwise good-humored Uncle Jim, "you are attacking my principles," and everyone puts down his glass and looks grave.

Now King Boruba's principles were three in number, and when

you have heard them you will say to yourself: "So *those* were the principles of King Boruba!"

There was the game of "Jack, Where Are You?" which was played at exactly four o'clock in the afternoon. It was of the greatest importance to abide by all the rules of the game: the counters, the velvet box they were kept in (they were not kept in the satin box), the ginger nuts, the Minister for Home Affairs in one corner of the room with a blindfold—all that seems highly entertaining to us today but that *then* was a principle, a genuine principle and not to be sneezed at. Anyone who played badly was suspect and anyone who couldn't play fled the country.

The second principle was the procession at five. It lasted only a quarter of an hour, down the beech avenue, around the pond and back again, finished, done, but it was still a principle. The people would stand waiting, twenty rows deep, and as the procession passed they all raised their hats at half-arm's length and shouted "Hurrah!" at exactly the same time. The king, leaning back in his ermine cloak, thought it was lovely, so he believed that others must find it lovely too. But the *princess* thought it dreadful; she sat stiffly in the carriage, blushing with shame, and counted the minutes on her fingers, one, two, three, to fifteen, and then it was over.

Of course you must hear about the princess. Her name was Steppie; it's very tiresome, I would rather she had been called Beatrice, or Evangeline, or some other name which is delightful for a storyteller to write, but there are no two ways about it, there's nothing to be done. Because when King Boruba, who wanted an heir, heard that a daughter had been born, he ran out and stood on the step, screaming and stamping his foot until the worst of his rage was over. And since then she had been called Steppie.

Steppie's life was not a happy one; her mother died when she was three, and since she had no brothers or sisters, she was obliged every day to sit alone with her father at table, in a great, cold hall. That was no joke. Because of his stomach the king could only eat pea soup, and so the whole court ate nothing but pea soup all the year round. That was the third principle. On New Year's Eve, when everyone else was eating fritters at midnight with happy smiles on their faces, the sighing courtiers stirred their 365th bowls of pea soup and put the spoons to their mouths with closed eyes. Pea soup was good for the stomach. To tell the truth, they cheated a bit; everyone had a slice of sausage or a hot roll tucked up his sleeve and when the master of ceremonies wasn't looking he would take a quick bite. It wasn't much, but because it wasn't allowed it was twice as agreeable.

But poor Princess Steppie sat right opposite her father, and when-

ever she raised her timid eyes from the dish she looked straight into the suspicious face of King Boruba. "Well?" he would say. "Is there anything up?" and she would swallow obediently.

Now, whether because of the pea soup or because she was a real princess of the blood we do not know, but she became more beautiful every day. Every day when she drove out (along the beech avenue, around the pond and back again), the people said: "No, she cannot grow more beautiful! It is impossible to be more beautiful!"

And yet, scarcely credible as it is, the next day she had grown more beautiful: her mouth a little redder, her hair silkier, her eyes more brilliant, her slender figure fairer yet.

But the mothers who stood by the wayside whispered: "How sad she looks! Never a smile on that sweet mouth! What can be going on in her little heart?" And the fathers growled: "It all comes of pea soup, wife! There's no need to look any further, it's simply the pea soup. No one could stand it forever, three bowls a day of it!"

The courtiers talked it over as well, but the king noticed nothing; he played the game of "Jack, Where Are You?", drove in his daily procession and was happy. Now, you know enough about the king and the princess to judge at their true value the events which were to occur. I have waited long enough, I can leave you in suspense no longer, however much I should like to; for it is a fearful—fearful!—thing to tell. There came a day—be on your guard!—when as the king rode out, the princess was so beautiful, sitting there blushing, with downcast eyes, that a butcher's boy could bear it no longer, jumped on the running board and gave her a smacking kiss!

The shock was tremendous. He was beheaded at once, converted into sausages in his former shop and thus put into circulation. But who can picture the sensation when the next day a greengrocer—someone from whom one would not expect such behavior at all—jumped on to the back of the carriage and gave the princess a loud kiss on the back of the neck! The king was completely stunned; he ordered the police to form a double line the next day, and they did. But one young policeman was unable to control himself and gave the princess a kiss with his helmet on. "Shame!" cried the king, and "Shame!" cried the old master of ceremonies, who was standing on the box. He had been at the job for sixty-seven years, but never before, he said, had he seen such a thing. Yet when he opened the carriage door to allow the princess to step out, he forgot his sixty-seven years' service, the three knightly orders on his coat and the medal for merit lying at home in a drawer, and gave her a kiss, kerplop! Yes, such things came to pass in those days. They do say that we are living in a peculiar age, but such things happened *then*.

The king at once summoned all his ministers, for, said he, this was no laughing matter. Nor did the ministers do so: they spent all Wednesday afternoon discussing it, and finally the Minister of Finance proposed that the procession be done away with. It would save money, too, he said. But the Minister of Education thought that would be a pity; divine nature was so instructive to the young.

"And what do you think?" the king asked the Minister for Home Affairs.

"Sire," said he, "she must marry."

"Whatever next?" said the king. "Marry? Do you mean it's not enough to have pea soup every day and 'Jack, Where Are You?' What else is there? Do *I* have more?"

"I am not unaware," said he respectfully, "that her position is a privileged one. On the contrary, your Majesty, on the contrary. But she is now twenty-five, and very beautiful. This has been established in an all too deplorable manner. What is more natural than for her to marry? It is entirely in accordance with the course of events! Once married, no butcher's boy will jump on to the running board, the processions can continue and I would also bring to your illustrious attention the chance of a successor to the throne."

"Hm," said the king. "I'll think about it."

Princess Steppie also lay in bed at night, thinking about it. A butcher's boy, a grocer, a policeman and a master of ceremonies had kissed her; could she really be beautiful? She got out of bed and looked at herself in the mirror. Dear God in Heaven, help us! Was that really she? What glorious brown hair, what great, dark eyes! And suddenly, for the first time in her life, she began to cry bitterly; it was as if all the stored misery became too much for her little heart and burst forth in wild, ungovernable sobs. She could not tell why, and that was the worst thing of all.

"Hey, there!" cried the king, looking around the door in surprise. "What is the meaning of this? No silliness, I hope? What's it all about?"

"I don't know, father," said the princess, sobbing, "I—I really don't know . . ." and she burst into tears all over again.

"I don't know, I don't know," repeated the king peevishly. "There is a reason for everything. Was the pea soup too hot? Didn't you enjoy the ride? Did you lose at the game?"

"N-no, Father . . ."

"Well, then," said the king, "everything is all right. Go to bed, and not another sound. It's much too noisy for me. For shame!"

King Boruba pulled the door shut; but in the passage he suddenly remembered his conversation with the minister. So he turned back and put his head around the door again. "There," he cried, "it's true! You're getting married!"

The princess lifted her tear-stained face; an inexplicable feeling overwhelmed her. "I, Father?"

"Yes, you. You are twenty-five, and—well, it's the natural course of events! No more butcher's boys will jump on the running board, the processions will go on, and the chance of a successor to the throne has been brought to my attention."

"I would like to," said the princess, blushing, "as long as it's a *nice* man."

"That is my business," said the king. "I shall choose him."

And that was what the king did. He wrote off to the other kings, inviting them to send their eldest sons along, because his daughter was to marry and it was always convenient to have a choice—yes, that was his honest way. There were exactly twenty letters and, mark well, he posted them on Sunday and by Monday the twenty princes were sitting in the waiting-room giving each other suspicious glances, so beautiful was the princess. The king left them waiting for an hour, then ascended his throne and cried: "Come in!" In came the first prince; he stood strictly to attention and waited quiveringly for the questions the king was going to put to him.

"Ah," said the king graciously, "sit down. Do you like pea soup?"

"No," said the prince quickly.

"Off you go, then," said the king. "I find people who don't care for pea soup quite ridiculous."

The second prince didn't like pea soup either and the third said it made him sick. The fourth couldn't bear the sight of it. The fifth—ah, he was a good prince! His eyes were just like those malted milk balls you see in some candy stores—three cents apiece or four for a dime, dark brown and shining, speckled with light. Hundreds of curls sprang forth under the band of his cap; yes indeed, he was a good prince! And he was well-mannered too! He bowed as if his waist were made of elastic, looking at the princess the while with such lovelorn eyes that her heart was pierced through and through. "Do you like pea soup?" asked the king.

"I'm mad about it, your majesty," said the prince, surprised. "There is nothing I like so much."

"Oh, Father," whispered the princess, "let's have him!"

"Tut, tut," said the king, "he has good taste, but what about his general education? Do you know the game of 'Jack, Where Are You?' "

The prince stared at the ceiling. "No," he said at last, "I don't know it."

"Next!" shouted the king.

But the next didn't know it either, and still less the one after.

"Strange," said the king. "Remarkable! At first sight they look intelligent and amiable. But as soon as you really go into the matter, you begin to see what they're worth. Hey, nonny no! How many are there to come?"

"Thirteen, Sire," said the Lord Chamberlain.

"Let all thirteen of them in," the king commanded. "I can't be bothered with such nincompoops one at a time."

Click, clack, there the thirteen stood, straight as candles.

"Do you like pea soup?" cried the king.

"No, Sire!"

"About, turn!" ordered the master of ceremonies.

And they were gone.

"Now, dear Father," said the princess that evening at dinner, "where is the husband you have chosen for me? Let him come in, I long so much to see him, I long so—" and at this she began to cry.

"Foolish child," said the king, "why start crying now? I'll find him, you shall see. I could do nothing with those blockheads who came this afternoon. Their taste was coarse and strange, and their education . . . my God! They couldn't answer the simplest things, things which everyone should know. But be patient! It will be all right!"

But it was not all right. All the princes who came were sent away. One didn't care for pea soup, another didn't know the game of "Jack, Where Are You?" and a third didn't enjoy processions in the afternoon.

So the princess who wanted so much to get married, did not marry. She grew more silent than before and one day she was dead. That's right, dead. The king was very much surprised; he simply did not understand how anyone who had pea soup every day and played the game of "Jack Where Are You?" could go and die. But dead she was, so he walked wonderingly behind her coffin to the cemetery. Ding! Dong! chimed the bells and the princess dropped at the end of four thick ropes into a deep hole where she still lies. And when the king also died a year later (for even kings do die), there was no heir. The kingdom went to the dogs, the palace fell into ruin and everything was over. And on the place where it once stood there is now a great stretch of sand where the children bake cakes on Sundays and now and then find a soup bowl.

But no one knows where these come from, and almost every day another professor publishes another book about it. But no one asks the story-teller. He does not count.

Maraboe
and
Morsegat

IN Finland, you must know, they have the naughtiest children. There are naughty children in other countries, of course, but the naughtiest of all live in Finland. And even in Finland there are two children who are naughtier than all the *other* naughty children. It is a strange thing, but every year the two naughtiest used to disappear. No one knew how, but it happened. This had been going on for six years, and no mortal man knew what had become of the six-times-two naughtiest children. They were never found again. In fact, people did not bother themselves too much about it. They searched, of course, because it is not very nice to do nothing at all about lost people, but they soon went back to work, thinking to themselves: "We are well rid of them!" Only the father and mother were heartbroken. And now it was the seventh year.

The two naughtiest children that year were a brother and sister called Maraboe and Morsegat. Their parents were good people. They lived in a great wood full of ghosts. There were witches and fairies there, too, and the bark of the trees formed strange faces that stuck out their tongues when you were not looking.

"How are we to keep them from going into the wood?" said the children's father, "If we forbid it, they will do it at once."

His good wife considered. "It is quite simple," she said. "They never do what we say. So if we say that they can go into the wood, then they will not go."

No sooner said than done. "Look here, children," said the father, "we would very much like you to go into the wood. It is a magic wood full of terrible wizards and dreadful old witches. You can't trust your life there. Now, you would be giving us great pleasure if you went into the wood. Oh, how happy we should be!"

The good man really meant it a little bit, for he had almost had enough of his naughty children. He was very poor and they broke everything in the house.

"We're not going," said Maraboe.

"We'll never go," said Morsegat.

The good man took out his handkerchief and began to weep bitterly.

"Just once," he sobbed, "to please me."

"Now we really won't go at all!" they shouted.

Their father dried his tears and nodded to his wife.

"Come with me, mother," he said, "we'll go into the next room, and cry a little."

They slipped away on tiptoe, but no sooner had they shut the door than they clasped one another about the waist and danced round the room. Now, in the door was a hole which Maraboe had cut. He looked through and saw his two good parents dancing merrily.

"Morsegat!" he cried. "Go away, and *don't* look through this hole!" for he knew that his sister would come and do just that at once. Morsegat looked, and then they both realized that they had been tricked.

"We'll go now," said Maraboe.

"And without our coats and gloves," said Morsegat, "for they don't like that."

The children ran bareheaded into the wood. It was deep winter and bitterly cold. The snow floated down in thick flakes and the breath came out of the children's mouths like two plumes of smoke. There were strange faces in the bark of the trees, and when Maraboe whirled round quickly one of them had its tongue out.

"But we'll go on," said Maraboe.

"Just because we're not allowed to," said Morsegat.

They walked and walked and the wood grew darker and darker. The branches creaked and white clouds scudded through the tree tops. In the trunk of an old oak a door opened slowly and through the gap another pair of glittering eyes peered at them. Then the door closed with a slam.

"Morsegat," said Maraboe, "this wood is enchanted."

"Yes," said Morsegat, "and do you know how you can tell? By the snow. Just open your mouth."

Maraboe opened his mouth wide and let the flakes blow in.

"You are right," he said, "it is sugar."

They grabbed handfuls of snow from the ground and ate sugar until they could eat no more.

"Now we must try the trees," said Morsegat.

They broke off a twig and munched.

"Chocolate!" they cried. "Now let's try the toadstools."

All the toadstools were made of toffee and the ground itself was made of fudge. And the nice thing was that all the trees had a different taste. The pliant alderwood was made of gingerbread and an old elm of chocolate mousse.

"They always say you come to a bad end if you are disobedient," said Morsegat, "but this whole wood is made of good things to eat. So it's all stuff and nonsense."

No sooner had she said this than a little old woman appeared from behind a tree. She was leaning on a stick and in her other hand she carried a great key.

"Good day, children," she said, in a croaking voice. "Going for a walk in Lollipop Land?"

"None of your business, old witch," replied Morsegat.

"Now I know!" said the old woman delightedly, "you are this year's two naughtiest children! I have been looking for you for days. You cannot come with me to my little house."

"Then we will come!" cried Maraboe.

"Quite so," muttered the old woman gleefully, "just as I thought." And she turned and hobbled quickly away.

Very soon they saw the old witch's house between the trees. She put the key in the lock and opened the door. Then she stood in the doorway and said:

"I would be very upset if you went in. But I am only an old woman and I cannot prevent you."

The children ran headlong past her and rushed into the house. It had three little rooms and a kitchen. The floors were brightly polished and the white curtains at the windows were freshly ironed. The copper pans in the kitchen shone and the tables gleamed so brightly that you could see your face in them. There was no dust on the chairs and, though the windows were firmly barred, the bars gleamed as if they were made of gold. The witch turned the key three times in the lock and dropped it into the pocket of her black apron.

"There we are," she said. "You will never get out again."

The children stared at her, open-mouthed.

"Well, isn't it nice here, eh?" cackled the old witch. "I used to do

all this work, but it was beginning to bore me. From now on, *you* will be doing it."

"Give me that key!" shrieked Maraboe.

"Come and get it," the witch replied.

The boy sprang at her and burrowed in the pocket of her apron. The next minute he was holding a coal-black snake in his hand. The creature hissed and coiled itself about his fingers.

"One of my little talents," explained the witch. "This snake is harmless, but if you try again you will find a poisonous one. Look, here is another key. Now pay attention, for I am going to hang it on this nail on the wall. Now, you will be thinking: we can easily get that down. All right, just try."

The children did not move. They were frightened now.

"That was just as well," said the witch, "for whoever touches the key turns into a black cat. Now, off to bed! In the morning I will come and wake you up at six and then you will work all day long."

She pushed the children up a narrow stairway, but she herself remained below. She lighted a candle and read in her book of spells.

In the attic the children looked fearfully about. It was full of cobwebs and in the middle of the room were two little beds. But what surprised the children most was the number of black cats. There were twelve altogether. They were lying on the beds and sitting on the beams and they began to mew pitifully. They all jumped down at once and wove their black bodies about the children's legs, as if they were trying to say something.

"Oh, Maraboe," whispered Morsegat, "do you remember what the witch said? Whoever touches the key will be turned into a black cat! So we are not the first. Twelve other children have been here before us, and just look round you and see what happened to them! They all tried to take the key and they were all changed into black cats."

She had hardly spoken when all the cats began to mew again, as if to say: "Yes, you are right, but please help us!" Maraboe went to the attic window and looked out into the dark night. The snow had stopped and all the trees stood still and white in the moonlight. Far in the distance he could see the little lantern that burned at the door of their own home, but it was so dreadfully far away that he knew he could never find it again. And over the window was a strong copper grating, with bars as thick as the fingers of a full-grown man.

"Dear Morsegat," said Maraboe, "let us go to sleep. Where there's a will there's a way."

The little girl began to cry. And then her brother did something he had never done before. He put his arm around her shoulders and pulled her head against him. He kissed her and said: "Don't be sad, for if we love one another we are certain to get out of here."

And at that moment the witch's candle began to gutter and went out. The letters in the book of spells danced before her eyes and the key fell off the nail and clattered to the ground. The witch jumped, for she knew that somehow her power had been weakened. She quickly hung the key on the wall and relighted her candle. And then she ran upstairs to see what had happened. But the two children were lying in bed, sleeping like babies. The cats, however, arched their backs and spat. The witch shook her fist.

"Just you wait, black cats," she muttered, "there will be two more of you soon."

A hard time began now for Maraboe and Morsegat. Every morning at six o'clock the witch woke them from their sleep with a stick and screamed: "Get up, you lazy rascals, and down you go!" They had to scrub and sweep and polish all day and the witch crawled about on her knees with a magnifying glass to see if there was any dust left on the floor. Maraboe also had to clean the copper grating, polish the windows and scour the pans until they were as bright as mirrors. Morsegat had to stoke the furnace and cook the meal.

The witch ate the strangest food. Stuffed stinging nettles with toadstools for breakfast, boiled thistles and grass for lunch and for supper a gigantic bowl of soup made of strange weeds. Worst of all, the children had exactly the same to eat. They grew thinner and thinner and looked more and more anxiously at the key on the wall. That was exactly what the witch wanted. "Go on," she said, "take it! You easily could, couldn't you?"

One night Maraboe sat on Morsegat's bed as his sister slept.

"Wake up, Morsegat," he said, "and look at that crack in the floor."

Morsegat rubbed her eyes and saw a glimmer of light from the room below.

"Shall we have a look?" asked Maraboe.

At this all the cats began to purr loudly. "That's a good sign," said Morsegat, and she jumped out of bed at once and peeped through the crack. She was just above the witch and looked straight into her book. But she had been so lazy at school that she had not learned to read.

"Oh, what a shame," she said, with tears in her eyes. "If only I had paid more attention to my lessons."

"Patience," said Maraboe, "we can make up for it now."

So every night they worked hard remembering letters and words and after three months they really could read the book.

They read what you have to do to turn a mouse into a toadstool and what you must say to turn a toadstool back into a mouse. They learned the spell that turns a child into a white swan, and how to fly through the air on a broomstick. They also read what rhyme you have to say to turn into a rabbit and what herbs you must eat to become completely invisible. They learned how to stay under water without drowning and how to go through fire without getting burned. And they read that you could make a tree hollow by running three times round it at full moon, and that the wind would change direction if you lay with your left ear on the moss. Finally they read that every year the witch enticed the two very naughtiest children into the wood and made them work in her house for a whole year. And when the year was over she turned the two children into black cats and lured two more children to her house. When they read that, they were very frightened.

"How long have we been here?" asked Morsegat.

"Tomorrow it will be a year," replied Maraboe.

When he said this, all the cats began to mew softly. The children looked at one another and they were both thinking the same thing. For now they knew enough to become birds and fly through the grating or to turn into mice and slip out under the door. But they did not want to leave the other poor creatures behind.

"No," said Morsegat, "we won't do that."

"Never," said Maraboe. "Out together and home together!"

And once again the witch's candle flickered and the key clattered to the floor. This time she was even more startled. She put the key in her black apron and slipped up the stairs on tiptoe. But the children were sleeping like babies. The cats were purring, however, until the attic hummed with the sound. The witch shook her fist.

"Just wait, black cats," she muttered. "There will be two more of you tomorrow."

Next day the children had to work harder than ever. The witch hit and beat them to her heart's content and even crawled with her magnifying glass under the cupboard to see if there was a speck of dust to be found. At last, when the afternoon was beginning to grow dark, she took her stick and said:

"I'm going out now. When I come back I shall have two children with me. So see to it that the meal is on the table." She seized the key from its hook and turned it three times in the lock behind her. Then off she went into the wood. At once Maraboe flew up the stairs and looked out of the attic window.

"I see two children in the distance!" he cried. "What shall we do now?"

"Look in the book," said Morsegat. "There is no time to be lost!"

They flew to the book and began to turn the pages. They knew it almost by heart, but at the very end, on the last page of all, there was something they had never read. It was the page that the witch never opened, for on it were secret spells which she herself did not fully understand and which her grandmother on her father's side had written in her own handwriting. The letters were written in blood and the cats spat nervously when they saw the red writing. But the children began to read. They read that when you meet a witch with two children you must seize her stick and put it over her left shoulder. Then she will instantly turn into a black crow.

"Quick!" cried Morsegat, "we'll read the rest later! There they are already!"

She looked through the window and there was the witch, hobbling back. She had two children with her, a boy and a girl, who were mocking and jeering at her.

"You wicked old hag!" cried the boy. "Why *can't* we go into your house?"

"I would rather you didn't!" quavered the witch. "I wouldn't like it at all!"

"Then that's what we'll do," cried the girl, "if only to spite you!"

The witch sighed and turned the key three times. The lock was heavy and she had to use both hands. When the door swung open she tried to pick up her stick again but Maraboe had already seized it. As quick as a flash he put the stick over the witch's left shoulder and closed his eyes tightly. When he opened them again a crow was flying over the tree-tops, cawing loudly, and as he watched, it vanished through the misty air.

"Run as fast as you can!" he shouted to the new children. "Run for your lives!"

The four of them rushed into the wood and the twelve cats sped silently behind them. When they reached a clearing they stopped.

"Here is the book," panted Morsegat, for she had snatched it up as they went. "We must read more of the last page. And we must hurry, for I see the crow coming back!"

The black bird was already hunting through the grey mist and descending in wide circles towards them. It was difficult to find the spell to change black cats back. It was the most secret spell in the whole book and it was at the very bottom of the page, in very small letters, just when you really thought there was nothing more to come. And this was the spell:

> "Greasy mash and mushy grout,
> Wring the spotted dishcloth out!"

As soon as Maraboe had read the words aloud an icy wind blew through the wood and, at the same instant, twelve more children were standing there. And down from the sky fell the crow, stone dead on the ground. The sixteen children took each other by the hand and marched singing through the wood. And so they all returned to their parents.

How happy their fathers and mothers were! They wept for joy and could not believe their eyes, for all the children (even the two latest ones) had become good. They made their own beds, they helped to wash up in the evening and put out the rubbish bins in the morning of their own accord, without being asked. That was nothing to them, after the things they had had to do for the witch all year long! They ate everything that was put on their plates, and even when it was not particularly tasty they thought it wonderful. Their fathers and mothers sometimes grew quite anxious and coaxed them: "You can be a little less good if you like!" but being nice came naturally to the children now, and they could not stop.

So if you go to Finland you will be in the next-best-behaved country in the world. The best-behaved, of course, is *this* one.

The Soldier
with the
Wooden Leg

ONCE upon a time there was a soldier who had nothing to do, for the war was now over. He went to the king and presented arms.

"King," he said, "here I am."

"So I see," said the king, "and what can I do for you?"

"I have always served you faithfully," said the soldier. "When there was fighting I was to be found in the front ranks. See, I have only one leg left."

The king looked. And in fact the soldier was standing on one leg.

"Lost," said the soldier, "for king and country."

"Soldier," said the king, "I shall not forget."

"It was a pleasure," replied the soldier. "And now, where is the enemy?"

"The enemy is defeated," said the king, "and the land is at peace. Can you not understand that?"

"Oh, yes," replied the soldier, "but I am a fighting man. Show me the enemy and you will see what I am still good for."

The king considered. "Listen," he said, "the palace is haunted and no one gets a wink of sleep at night. Could you do something about that?"

The soldier spat on the ground. "No such things as ghosts," he said. "I thought you had more sense than that."

"That's what I like to hear," said the king happily. "You can spend the night here, for the ghost comes on only one night a week, and tonight is the night. If you catch him you will get a plate of soup and the privilege of standing guard at the gates."

"Good," said the soldier. "And what shall we wager?"

Now the king was a thrifty man. "If you catch him, you can keep

37

him," he said. "But if you do not succeed, you shall stand guard for nothing and get not a penny in pay."

The soldier agreed, for he simply wanted to make a wager about something. He stumped along on his wooden leg to the room where the ghost always walked. The attendants locked the door firmly behind him, for no one wanted to have anything to do with the ghost. The soldier sat down in the dark and filled his pipe. He was a carefree fellow and he thought the whole business stuff and nonsense.

When twelve o'clock struck, a faint wailing sound arose and the room turned icy cold. The soldier stood up and knocked out his pipe. "It's a bit chilly in here," he said. "I'll put on my coat." He went to the hook where his coat was hanging, but no sooner had he put it on than the windows began to rattle and a weird, greenish light filled the room.

"At least I can see something now," said the soldier, pulling out his watch. "Five past twelve. The ghost is five minutes late."

The words had scarcely left his mouth when the ghost appeared. He came straight through the locked door and stood in front of the soldier. The soldier nodded.

"You're late," he said. "Couldn't you come on time?"

The ghost shook his head.

"I had to terrify an old woman on the way," he said softly.

He had a strange, hollow voice, as if he were speaking inside a barrel, and the curious thing was that his lips did not move as he spoke. The soldier spat on the floor again, for he always did that when there was something he didn't like.

"Frightening old women!" he said scornfully. "I thought better of you. Aren't you ashamed?"

"No," said the ghost.

The soldier liked this.

"You're an honest fellow, anyway," he said. "And now I shall cut off your head, for you are the king's enemy."

"Try it," replied the ghost.

"That I will!" cried the soldier, and he drew his sword to slice the ghost's head from its body with one blow, for he could do that sort of thing—he was famous for it. But the sword passed straight through the ghost and the soldier fell flat on the floor.

"I am immaterial," said the apparition softly. "Didn't you know?"

The soldier stood up and dusted himself.

"No," he said. "You could have told me that before. What else can you do?"

"I can do everything," replied the ghost simply.

"I don't believe it!" cried the soldier.

Then the ghost grew angry. He radiated a greenish light and his whole form shuddered.

"Ask what you like," he said, quivering, "and I will do it."

"Good," said the soldier. "Do you see this bottle?"

"I see it," replied the ghost. "In fact I can see straight through it."

"That is not really very strange," said the soldier, "for it is glass. But can you get *into* it?"

The ghost laughed scornfully.

"I could do *that*," he said, "when I was still a child."

"Well," said the soldier, "one can forget these things."

Now the ghost was trembling so violently that the windows shook.

"Wretch!" he said in a hollow voice. "Do you know to whom you speak?"

And the next moment he was in the bottle. This was just what the soldier had been waiting for. Instantly he put in the cork and pulled the bellrope.

"Take me to the king," he said to the footman. "I have caught the ghost."

The king was already in bed when the soldier came to his room with the bottle.

"Well done," he said admiringly. "Let me have a close look at him —this is not something one sees every day."

And that was true, for the whole bottle was bright green and sparks were flying inside the glass, the ghost was so angry.

"He can't get out," said the king happily. "It is a great relief, because I could not shut my eyes as long as he was about. Soldier, you have done well. And you may keep him, too."

"Don't I get anything else?" asked the soldier.

"Nothing," replied the king, "for that was the wager. You're doing well, soldier. In the kitchen is a dish of soup and you can have the whole of it. Close the door quietly, please—I detest slammed doors." And the king turned over and went to sleep.

The soldier had experienced many things in the war, but now he stood there quite amazed. He waited a moment to see if the king would

say anything more, but the king was already snoring. Then the soldier spat on the floor and marched out of the palace. He did not look to right or left and when he reached his own little house he put the bottle in a cupboard and closed the door with a bang.

Times grew hard for the warrior now. People praised him because he had lost a leg for king and country, but they thought it a pity that there was only one left. "You're a hero," they said, "but a hero on one leg, and we cannot use such a man."

The soldier began to grow hungry. He stumped through the house, searching for something to eat. And suddenly he came upon the bottle.

"Let me out!" cried the ghost faintly.

"I know better than that," replied the soldier. "You are the only thing I have."

The ghost stood up and banged his fists against the glass.

"This is no life for me!" he cried piteously.

"You make things lively enough for others," replied the soldier. "What will you do for me if I let you out?"

"Everything," replied the ghost.

The soldier took a chair and sat before the bottle, for everything is a great deal.

"I can talk to you," he said. "I want to be king and reward all the soldiers who have lost a leg in the war."

"Nothing simpler," said the ghost. "You should have said so before. It shall be done, soldier, and now let me out."

"Ho ho, not so fast!" cried the soldier. "Once I believed everybody, but now I have more sense. *First* make me king and *then* you can come out."

The ghost stared glumly at the bottom of the glass bottle.

"Shouldn't we do it the other way around?" he asked. "It comes to the same thing, doesn't it?"

"Not at all," replied the soldier. "It makes all the difference. And if I had known that before, I would still be walking around on two legs. But just as you like. I can shut the cupboard again."

As he stood up to close the door, the ghost fell on his knees and clasped his hands imploringly. The whole cupboard turned bright green, for the little creature was radiating not only anger, but fear. "You shall be king, you shall be king!" he wailed. "Just look outside!"

The soldier looked out of the window and stiffened with amazement. There, up the narrow lane where he lived, marched a whole company of soldiers and each of them had only one leg. The noise of their wooden legs clattering on the cobbles was terrifying.

"You are our king!" they cried. "March to the palace with us and that will be the end of our troubles!"

The soldier stepped out among his comrades and for the first time he felt completely happy. As he marched he looked at the people who had the usual two legs and he felt himself growing happier and happier.

"They are men, too," he thought. "I will be good to them. Not everyone has been in the war and they cannot help it."

When they reached the palace gates the guard dropped his gun in a fright and ran away as fast as his two legs would carry him. And even the king, who happened to be looking out of the window at that moment, took to his heels through the back door of the palace. If one of those heels had been a wooden one, he would have stayed where he was, but he was frightened and tore across the fields as if the devil were after him. And that is the disadvantage of having everything.

So the soldier became king. He was good to the people with one leg and he had great sympathy for all the others.

"We must not be proud," he said to his soldiers, "and we must try not to put on airs. Ours is a privilege that is not granted to everyone, but we need not pat ourselves on the back, for all that."

And he did not do so, except when he was quite alone and no one could see him.

By royal command the ghost was let out of the bottle. He was allowed to haunt once a week and the new king sat by, smoking his pipe.

"Carry on, my lad," he said kindly, "haunt away! You are only young once."

This began to annoy the ghost, for it was not what he wanted. He gradually lost his green glow and in the end he was just an ordinary ghost, on two ordinary legs.

"I'm going," he said crossly. "This is no fun any more."

The king spat on the floor, for he could not drop the habit.

"A pity," he said. "I thought you had more sense. But go in peace."

And the ghost went. But the king remained. For he *had* more sense.

Anna

ON the sloping roof over the kitchen lay an egg. Oh, what a tiny little egg it was! It was much, much smaller than a button and only a storyteller could have seen it. But fortunately, the storyteller did see it. He was looking for his glasses; just then the egg opened and Anna came out. She walked across the left lens and looked at her reflection.

"Oh, is that me?" she cried in surprise. "How very nice!"

Yes, she was a mayfly. Anna took a deep breath and stared up at the church clock. It was eight o'clock in the morning.

"This is a precious day," said little Anna. "Today I must grow up, get engaged, marry, have children and die. By eight o'clock this evening all that must have happened. I feel rather short of courage, with so many things ahead of me. But nothing ventured, nothing gained!"

She spread her wings and fluttered bravely over the sundial. Here she met with a nice gentleman called Simon Upandown. He looked rather old, half a day at least, but well preserved. In fact Anna thought him very smart. And he was so discreet.

"Ah, young lady . . . ." was all he said.

Anna blushed.

"I have just been born," she said.

"Come, come," he said impatiently, "we musn't talk our time away. Yes or no?"

"Yes," said little Anna.

They embraced one another hastily and wandered off among the lettuces.

"Is this the wedding?" asked Anna shyly.

"Yes, this is it," said Simon.

He too glanced at the church clock.

"It is half past nine now," he said.

He turned pale and gave Anna a kiss. Then he lay down on his back, his feet in the air. He was dead. Anna was more surprised than depressed. She would really have liked to bury her head in the sand and have a good cry, but that was no way for a middle-aged woman to behave. Anna had grown up now and took a broader view of life. She was still thinking about it when her brothers passed: born in shadow, they had come into the world a little later. Anna stayed to watch the rest of the eggs hatching from a distance. She felt kindly towards them, even a little bit blasé.

"Life," she announced, "life, young people, is rapid disillusionment. Faster! Faster! That is all that is required of you."

But the little mayflies did not answer. They spread their little wings and flew straight up towards the sun. Anna took courage as well, jumped up and flew over the dovecote; there she met her second husband.

They became acquainted quite practically; poetry is ridiculous at their time of life.

"Have you been married before?"

"Oh, yes," said Anna, "it was a very nice marriage, but he passed away. It was the wrong time of day."

"Good. Do you feel inclined to marry again?"

"Whom?" asked Anna.

"Me."

"Oh, yes," said Anna.

With that they married. No, it could not have been quicker. And yet it was a long process, for a mayfly.

Was it a happy marriage? No. She suspected that he had a share in the affair of the ant-egg swindle, but there was no proof. However, he was caught smuggling a scrap of horse dung and arrested. The law is strict.

Anna did not grieve; she laid a couple of hundred eggs in the cup of a primula and allowed herself to float off on the wind.

Higher and higher she went. It was so blissful, this carefree drifting . . . suddenly Anna felt tired, teribly tired. She quickly spread her wings and alighted. Was this to be the end? Tears sprang into her eyes; she drank some water from a cabbage leaf and fell asleep.

When she awakened the sun was red and gloomy and everything in the garden had grown old and silent. Anna too was an old woman. She walked slowly across the cabbage leaf and sat down on the edge. From here she could watch the sun setting. Anna sighed and stared down over the edge of the leaf at the life going on beneath her.

Snails, bugs and beetles, creatures of all kinds were hurrying home. There was falling and getting up again, climbing and dropping, creeping and scrambling.

Only Anna did not move again.

The Rich Blackberry Picker

M ANY years ago there was an old blackberry picker who lived in a great wood. His father and mother had already lain buried at the foot of a beech tree for half a century, but the blackberry picker had long since forgotten all about that; he did not even know what the lopsided cross really meant, but thought it advisable, should he have to pass that way at night, to make a detour.

There was no one else living in the wood and so the blackberry picker thought he was alone in the world. However, this belief in no way affected his high spirits. He would sing the merriest songs at the top of his voice, without pause, except at night, because that was when he had to sleep—and that is a good excuse. But apart from that, it was impossible to imagine a happier man. "Look," he was wont to exclaim in the morning, "at the silvery beads on the flowers! For whom are all these diamonds strewn upon the grass, if not for me? How rich I am!" And when he was walking through the wood he would sigh: "What a lofty vault, what a spacious hall, what a splendid pillar! And all this for one man!" In the afternoons he would lie on his back gazing at the clouds, which put on a marvelous show for him. "Look," he would say, "a bear! And there's a winter landscape! Who else has such a ceiling? I find it quite embarrassing!" But the blackberry picker was happiest of all in the evenings. Then he would sit under the laurel tree in front of his house and wait excitedly. And suddenly, as the sun cast her last purple rays over the hills, a rich, high voice would begin to carol far away in the woods, so astoundingly beautiful and yet so infinitely melancholy that tears sprang into the blackberry picker's eyes. "Wonderful, splendid!" he would cry at last. "Thank you, thank you, unknown singer! What music! What a sound! How unfortunate that I am alone in the world!"

But he was not alone; one evening an explorer who was traveling through the wood pushed open the rickety little door and stood smiling at the blackberry picker. "Friend," said he, "some food and a bed, no more. For I am hungry and tired. Do you understand me?"

But the blackberry picker sat in his chair, pale as death, and said nothing.

"Come, come," the traveler went on, "here is a gold coin. That should loosen your tongue."

Up stood the blackberry picker. "Creature," he said painfully, "I do not need your gold. That is not why I was silent. But may I touch you?"

"Suit yourself," said the traveler, who was a jovial man.

So the blackberry picker felt the traveler; he pinched his nose, turned his head in all directions, gazed solemnly into his mouth and cried at last: "Just like me! Just like me! All the same!" and he embraced him.

"What a simpleton you are!" laughed the traveler, disengaging himself. "Have you never seen a human being before?"

"I am not alone!" cried the blackberry picker, clapping his hands. "I am not alone! Just the same legs!" and he danced around the table.

"Come," repeated the traveler, "I am hungry. Try to control yourself." He sat down at the table, took a plate from his rucksack and set it down in front of him with a suggestive clatter.

"Now then," he said, "let's be about it."

"Yes, yes," cried the blackberry picker, "just like me! Exactly the same!" And he danced to the store cupboard, fetched bread, sausage and honey cake and danced around the table with it all, at least three times. Then he sat down, took a deep breath and said: "Help yourself."

The traveler ate in silence. At every bite he took, the blackberry picker cried rapturously: "Just like me!" This was a little tiresome at first, but the traveler was hungry and he ate on, smiling. At last he raised his head; his eye fell on the gold piece lying there on the edge of the table.

"Friend," he said, "why would you not accept the coin from me?"

"I don't need it," the blackberry picker replied simply. "I have diamonds."

"Diamonds?" repeated the traveler. "*You* have diamonds? How many?"

"I don't know exactly," said the blackberry picker thoughtfully, "a few meadowsful."

"Say that again."

"A few meadowsful," repeated the blackberry picker.

This time it was the traveler who sat in his chair, pale as death.

"Man," he cried at last, "you are fabulously rich!"

"That's what I said," said the blackberry picker, "but that's not all. I've got plenty of other things besides."

"Tell me about them, comrade."

"Oh," said the blackberry picker awkwardly, "there's so much. There are the mirrors, for instance."

"Mirrors?" asked the traveler frenziedly.

"Yes," the blackberry picker continued in the same offhand tone, "a few thousand—I've never counted them. Some are so big you need a day to walk round them. Oh yes."

"A day to—friend, where are all these treasures?"

"In my house."

"It must be a palace!" stammered the traveler.

"It *is* a palace," the blackberry picker replied with a smile. "I've never seen the whole of it, it's too big. There are corridors of pillars so long you can't see the end of them; thousands of slender columns support the vault. They are a joy to behold! But here and there you come across wider halls; their vaults are not green but pale blue, with white flecks."

"You mean mosaic?" asked the traveler breathlessly.

"I don't know what that is," said the blackberry picker.

The traveler explained the difficult word.

"Oh, no," exclaimed the blackberry picker, laughing, "that's just child's play! That would end up by boring me: always looking at the same thing. No, here the shapes move, they pass slowly and steadily by, indeed they transform themselves into the most wonderful patterns: polar bears, winter landscapes and dwarves with beards. Even the colors change: first dark blue, then pale gray, sometimes both at the same time. It's exquisite to watch; you never get tired of it!"

"That is incredible!" cried the traveler. "Incredible! And all that for one man. But, but surely, you must sometimes feel lonely among all those pillars, galleries and mirrors?"

"Oh, no!" said the blackberry picker. "There is music enough, on all sides and all day long!"

"Music?" cried the traveler. "Music? Come, blackberry picker, you're making a fool of me now."

"No, really not," the blackberry picker assured him. "All day long, and the songs are always new. But the solos are sung in the evening; I have a special singer for those. You must listen tomorrow night. You'll be staying here tonight, of course?"

"No," said the traveler, pulling on his coat, "I'm going right off. I'm an explorer and this is my greatest discovery. I'm going to tell everybody."

"That you must," said the blackberry picker. "I have always felt guilty at having it all to myself. But do stay just one night. Then you can see everything for yourself tomorrow and will be the better able to talk about it."

"No," said the traveler, "time is money! I'm going right away. Thanks for the honey cake. Goodbye." He pulled the door shut behind him and vanished into the night. The blackberry picker hurried outside but saw only a shadow disappearing between the tree trunks.

"What a pity," he murmured, "time is money! And he could have had as many pearls as a man can carry. Traveler, traveler! Come back!"

But the traveler did not hear him; he was leaping over ditches and hedgerows, swimming two rivers, crossing a dark wood, and then he was in town.

"Mayor," said he, "I have something important to say."

"Well," said the Mayor, "that's nice. Go and stand on top of the Town Hall."

The traveler stood on top of the Town Hall.

"People!" he cried. "Would you be glad of some pearls?"

"Yes, indeed!" shouted the people.

"And does anyone care for mirrors, as big as this square?"

"Yes, indeed," said the people, "just give them to us!"

"And is there anyone here who would like to live in a palace with green colonnades and ceilings of moving mosaic?"

"We certainly would!" shouted the people. "Where is it?"

"Come with me!" cried the explorer. "Just follow right behind me! There is no time to be lost!"

So they passed through a dark wood, swam two rivers, leaped over ditches and hedgerows and came to the blackberry picker.

"Blackberry picker!" called the traveler. "Here we are!"

"How pleasant!" cried the blackberry picker. "You don't let the grass grow under your feet, I must say. Dearie me, what a lot of people you've brought with you! There must be easily a couple of thousand! What are you going to do?"

"We've come to get the pearls," said the Mayor, stepping forward, "and we're going to live in the palace where the ceiling is made of moving mosaic and the pillars are made of emerald. We have come to listen to the music, and we must have the mirrors, too."

"Well, that's splendid!" cried the blackberry picker, embracing him. "I'm so glad you appreciate it too! That you realize how beautiful it all is! Welcome, welcome! I haven't much honey cake, but there's plenty of good bread and fresh water."

"We don't want honey cake." The Mayor spoke slowly. "We want pearls."

"You shall have them!" cried the blackberry picker. "As many as you can carry. Wait till tomorrow."

"What about this evening?" asked the Mayor anxiously. "Time is money!"

"No," said the blackberry picker, shaking his head, "it's dark now. You can't see the pearls in the dark. But tomorrow morning early you shall see something! Get some sleep now, we have plenty of time."

"Right," said the Mayor. "Sleep, men! We have plenty of time!"

Next morning the fields lay glittering and sparkling under the rosy sky; on every blade of grass, even the smallest, hung magnificent, silvery diamonds, and when the sun had risen they changed into topazes, emeralds and blue sapphires, blazing with light, aflame with purity, more dazzling than earthly jewels. And the people stood among them, talking about the pearls which they were surely about to find, whole meadows full of them. If only the blackberry picker would wake up; they kept their eyes fixed on the little door.

At last it opened; the blackberry picker stepped out and gazed silently across the fields; his eyes were filled with tears. "You have been very lucky," he said softly.

"What did he say?" muttered the Mayor.

"I said: you have been very lucky," the blackberry picker repeated, smiling. "There have never been so many jewels before."

"I see no jewels," said the Mayor.

"You don't see any jewels?" asked the blackberry picker in surprise.

"We see nothing," cried the people, "we see nothing at all!"

The blackberry picker struck his hands together. "What bad eyesight you have!" he cried. "Look about you! Don't you see it?"

"That is dew," said the Mayor angrily.

"I—I didn't know," stammered the blackberry picker, "I thought—"

"Where are the colonnades?" asked the Mayor brusquely.

"There," whispered the blackberry picker.

"Those are trees," said the Mayor. "Where is the mosaic?"

"There," said the blackberry picker.

The mayor raised his eyes to the violet sky. "That is air," he said, "just air. Where are the mirrors?"

The blackberry picker pointed silently into the distance.

"Those are ponds," said the Mayor. "Where is the music?"

The blackberry picker lifted his forefinger; the Mayor listened. Then he straightened up and spoke with a bitter smile: "That is a nightingale, simpleton! A common nightingale! We have been deceived!"

"But I told it all just the way it is!" cried the blackberry picker. "I told it all . . ."

"Hang him!" shouted the people. "Let's hang him!"

And that evening when the nightingale began her throbbing song there was no one there to hear. For the blackberry picker was hanging on the next branch down, dead.

The Golden Slippers

LONG ago there lived a poor shoemaker, who longed to be rich. He was not old but he looked it. He lived in a little wooden house in the middle of the town, and every evening a gnome came to the house to eat his supper. On the stroke of six he rang the bell and walked in. The shoemaker set the gnome's dish on the table and put a thick book on the chair, for otherwise the little man could not have managed. He always ate the same thing: brown beans with bacon and a cup of coffee, which he drank from a thimble. When he had eaten and drunk he jumped down and made a little bow. "Many thanks," he said, "and goodbye until tomorrow." Then he vanished.

This had been going on for years. It did not cost the shoemaker much, since the gnome ate only three brown beans, which he cut in small pieces, and the bacon was no bigger than the scrap you would put in a mouse-trap.

But one evening the gnome did not go away when he had finished his meal. He sat behind his empty plate and gazed sorrowfully at the shoemaker. A great tear trickled down over his white beard.

"What is it?" asked the shoemaker. "Are you sad?"

"Yes," said the gnome. "I can never come here again."

The shoemaker was startled, for he had always enjoyed the gnome's company. "I was allowed to come for seven years," said the mannikin, "and now they are over. This is the last evening. Have you a wish?"

"Yes, indeed," said the shoemaker, "I would like to be very rich."

"Is that all?" asked the gnome. "Are you quite sure?"

"Quite sure," answered the shoemaker. "I have been longing for this for years."

The gnome sighed. "All right," he said, "so be it. It is a foolish wish, but a promise is a promise."

He stooped under the table and pulled off his two little slippers.

"Here," he said, "these are for you."

Then he jumped down from his stool and ran to the shoemaker in his stockinged feet. He flung his little arms round the cobbler's neck and kissed him on both cheeks.

"My heartiest thanks for all the good food," he said, "and if you ever need me, just call me. Farewell!"

The gnome was already at the door when the cobbler asked:

"How am I to call you?"

"Blow the whistle," answered the gnome.

"What whistle?"

"The one I have just pushed into your bag," said the gnome, and was gone.

The cobbler felt in his bag, and truly there was a little whistle in it. He blew on it once. The gnome put his head round the door and said:

"Because it is you, I won't count that one against you. But you must blow on it only when you really *need* me." And then he vanished in earnest.

"That's a fine thing," said the cobbler grumpily. "Two old slippers which would fit no one and a worthless whistle—what sort of reward is that for seven years' food? That will never make me rich!"

But in this he was mistaken. The very next day when he was about to throw the worn slippers into the dustbin, he found that one was full of silver coins, while the other was full of pieces of gold.

"Hallo!" cried the shoemaker. "This is a different story!"

He went to the tailor and bought a coat of gold brocade, breeches with silver buckles and a cap with peacocks' feathers. He emptied the slipper full of silver coins out onto the counter and at once the little shoe was full again.

"This is fine!" cried the shoemaker, setting off at once for the coachmaker's. He looked young and smart in his new clothes.

"I want a coach of pure gold," he said, "and the spokes of the wheels must be set with diamonds."

The coachmaker opened his eyes wide, but he did his best and within the space of two weeks the golden coach with the diamond wheels was rolling up the alley where the shoemaker lived. People came out of their houses to stare at the carriage, but they had to shield their eyes with their hands because the jewels glittered so brightly in the sun.

"Beautiful," said the shoemaker, "and how much will that cost me?"

"I am sorry to say it," replied the coachmaker, "but that is a costly carriage. A hundred sacks of gold for the materials, and ten sacks of silver for the work. If it suits you, so much the better, for I cannot change it."

"Come in, come in!" cried the shoemaker, and he emptied out one of the slippers until he had a hundred sacks of gold, and then the other for the ten sacks of silver.

"Now for the horses!" he cried, and bought himself four splendid white horses, whinnying to be off; he hired a coachman and took on a footman as well, who had to stand behind the carriage, in a velvet cap and shoes with silver buckles.

"Forward!" cried the cobbler. "Drive on!"

And the coach went down the lane and across country to the king's palace. The king was sitting by his window when he saw the carriage stop before the door.

"Great heavens," said the king. "Who can that be?"

He opened the door at once and the shoemaker stepped out of the coach.

"King," he said, "I am the richest man in the land."

"That cannot be," said the king, "for I am he."

"Shall we bet on it?" asked the cobbler.

"All right," said the king, "what shall we bet?"

"Listen," said the shoemaker, "have you any daughters?"

"Yes, indeed," answered the king, "I have three of them. The first is the loveliest, the second is the richest and the third is the sweetest."

"Then we'll compete for the richest," said the shoemaker delightedly. "Just tell me what I must do."

"I will tell you," said the king. "You must build a palace twice as big as mine. The walls must be of marble, the windows of mirror glass, the roof and gutters of copper. Can you do that?"

"Nothing simpler," answered the cobbler. "When must it be finished?"

The king smiled craftily.

"Tomorrow morning after breakfast," he said. "And if it is not ready I will cut off your head."

The cobbler was taken aback, for money can buy everything except time. He stepped into his carriage and drove through the city. He called on all manner of people, masons, glassblowers and plumbers, but they all shook their heads.

"We know our trade," they said, "but even if you gave us the slippers themselves, we could not perform miracles."

The cobbler was sitting disconsolately in his carriage, when he suddenly came upon the little whistle.

"This time I really do need him," he thought, and blew. And instantly one of the golden doors of the carriage opened and the gnome jumped in.

"You don't have to tell me," said he, "for I know everything already. Just go to sleep and look out of the window tomorrow morning."

The cobbler drove back to the palace and slept like a baby. And next day, when he got up and looked out of the window, he saw across the road another huge palace, of shining marble, with windows of mirror glass and a roof of copper. The king was still at breakfast when the cobbler went in. He regarded the cobbler smugly, for he had not looked out of the window.

"Good morning, shoemaker," he said. "You will lose your head today."

"Good morning, king," said the shoemaker. "Take a look outside."

The king looked out and froze in his chair.

"Great heavens," he whispered to himself. Then he called his servant and said: "Bring my richest daughter here."

But when the princess came in, the shoemaker turned as white as a sheet, for he had never seen anything so ugly in his life. She was short and squat and had a hump on her back. She squinted and her nose was so crooked that she could kiss the tip of it herself. And that was the only good thing about it, for no one else would do so. The cobbler looked down at his two little slippers in dismay. Money can do many things, but it cannot make an ugly girl beautiful.

"I really meant the *other* daughter," he said, "the most beautiful one."

"All right," said the king. "But in that case we shall have to start over again from the beginning. If you want the most beautiful daughter, then I want a more beautiful palace. That one across the street will have to go. It is very nice, but it could be much better. I would like to see one three times as big as mine. The walls must be of alabaster, the windows of crystal, the roof and gutters of silver. Can you do that?"

"Nothing simpler," answered the shoemaker. "When must it be ready?"

The king rubbed his hands together gleefully.

"Tomorrow morning after breakfast," he said, "and if it is not there, you will lose your head."

But this time the cobbler did not worry at all. He went into the park which lay round the palace and hid under a weeping willow whose branches swept the ground. There he blew his whistle. The leaves were pushed aside and there stood the gnome.

"You don't have to tell me," said he, "for I know everything already. Go off to sleep, and look out of the window in the morning."

And everything happened just as before. Only this time the palace was three times as big. People stood gazing at it in silence, for the walls were of finely-veined alabaster, the windows of glittering crystal and the silver roof shone so brightly that it hurt one's eyes.

The king was also standing looking out of his window when the shoemaker arrived.

"Neatly done, shoemaker," he said with satisfaction. "And now you shall have what I promised you."

Then he called his servant and commanded:

"Bring my most beautiful daughter here."

But when the princess crossed the threshold it was just as if an icy wind had blown through the room. She was stiff-necked and haughty and the shoemaker shivered when he looked into her chilly eyes. Her glance was hail and snow, her mouth bitter and her heart of stone. The cobbler looked at his two slippers, but they could not help him. You can do many things with money, but you cannot make a cold girl warm.

"Actually," he said, "I meant the *third* daughter, the sweetest of them."

"You can have her," said the king, "but not just for the asking. Now I want a palace seven times as large as mine. The walls must be of mother-of-pearl, the windows of diamond, the roof and gutters of pure gold. Can you do that?"

"My head upon it," said the shoemaker excitedly, "if it is not there by morning."

And he crawled under the old willow again and blew on his little whistle.

"You don't have to tell me," said the gnome, "for I know everything already. When you look out of the window tomorrow, you will see the palace there, all ready for you, but you have whistled for me three times now and you may not do it again. This is the very last time. I shall never come back." The mannikin swept off his cap, bowed and vanished.

Next morning the people streamed in their thousands to the place where the third palace was to rise from the ground. There! Even from a distance they could see the golden roof shimmering against the blue sky. The walls were of mother-of-pearl and every window was cut from a single diamond. Even the king could not believe his eyes, and stood open-mouthed by the window.

"Boy," he said, "bring my sweetest daughter here."

The girl entered shyly. Timidly she raised her dark lashes and looked at the shoemaker.

"Who is this, father?" she asked in surprise.

"Dearest daughter," said the king, "this is your husband."

The princess blushed and the cobbler fell in love with her at once. He stretched out his arms and cried: "And you are my wife!"

"I would like to be married," said the princess, "but I would like to know to whom."

"He is the richest man in the whole world," answered the king. "He just throws money away!"

The princess took the down-at-heel slippers and looked curiously at them.

"You can do many things with money," she said, "but you cannot buy happiness. Tell me what *you* have done with it?"

So the shoemaker told her he had spent it on a golden coach, a footman and a coachman, four white horses and the splendid clothes he had on.

"Then you have done nothing with it," answered the princess, "for all that was done for yourself. Did you not think of others at all?"

Now it was the cobbler's turn to look shamefaced.

"No," he said honestly, "not for a moment."

"And the little whistle," asked the princess, "what did you do with that?"

And the shoemaker told her that he had built three palaces with it for a wager, of which two had already been destroyed, and that he could never blow it again. The princess looked at him sorrowfully with her great eyes and even the king looked grave.

"So the whistle is no longer worth a whistle," he said, displeased.

"No," the shoemaker admitted, "but I still have my slippers!"

"That is true," said the princess, "and now you must choose.

Either you keep the slippers and I will not become your wife, or you throw them into the fire at once—and then I will go with you."

The cobbler seized the two slippers and flung them straight into the fire, for that was the sort of man he was. And at the same instant they heard a tremendous crash outside, as if a great building had fallen to the ground. And so it had. The place where the palace had stood was empty. Nothing was left but a wooden fence around the space.

"That's a fine thing!" cried the king. "Now you have nothing at all!"

But he was wrong about that. For when he turned around he saw that the cobbler had his daughter in his arms. She kissed him and cried: "Now I can see that you really love me! I will go with you to the end of the world!"

And they went out hand in hand through the front door and straight to the cobbler's little house. There they lived happily for a long time. And when the king died, the cobbler's wife became queen, for she was the eldest daughter.

She ruled the land wisely while her husband grew roses in the garden. Sometimes, seeing him so hard at work, the people said that he was hen-pecked, but he did not give a whistle for their talk. And the man who can say that is truly happy.

Happy Hughie

NOW this is the story of Happy Hughie, or how the Laughwort began. The Laughwort, or *herbus risus,* as the scholars say, grows only in our country, just as all plants grow where they are most needed. Together with its little sister, the Sneezewort, it belongs to the Ranunculacea family. And what a family that is! These are among the flowers which, if they were human beings, would be called the comfortable middle class: early to rise, cropping up everywhere. Scarcely had the young spring sun pressed her first shy maiden kiss upon the earth when—hoopla! there was the Sneezewort, the first up, looking about in amazement. And on St. Egbert's Day it was already pushing through the vines with its wonderful red flowers. As soon as you sniff it you begin to sneeze at once. "Bless you!" say the farmers, showing their large teeth.

Yes, the Sneezewort is a wonderful thing. But the Laughwort is still more wonderful; when you smell that you begin to laugh, and that is not the same as sneezing. Anyone can sneeze, it happens every day. But laughing is the greatest gift that God has given to poor man, a royal gift, which will forever distinguish him from the rest of creation. That is why there are only two things which make him laugh: a good conscience and—the Laughwort. If you want to find out about the first you will have to read it in a different book, a book which was written long before my time. But the Laughwort, ah, anyone who wants to find out about that must go to the storyteller. So let us hear about the Laughwort, how it began and whence it came. Listen well, so that you don't forget.

In a certain kingdom of Tuba, not far from here, lived the Tubanters. They were grave, good people. One made cheese, another sausages, a third sold eggs and altogether they lived well—one might even say, richly. And that was why foreigners looked in from time to time to clap their hands at the well-being, the decency and order in their country. "Superb!" they cried. "It is truly miraculous!"

"And yet," they would add after a little thought, "there is something missing. We don't know what."

There was one foreigner who did know. "You Tubanters," he said, "are essentially a grave and sober people. Everything here is neat and tidy and all that one could wish. But tell me, don't you ever do anything silly? Don't you ever make jokes?"

"Jokes?" said the Tubanters. "No. All we make is cheese and sausages. We don't make jokes. How do you do that?"

The stranger began to laugh. "Look here!" he said, and he smacked his knee, danced in a circle, told many jokes and roared with laughter. But the Tubanters looked on gravely until he had finished and then asked: "Have you been making jokes?"

"Oh yes," said the stranger.

"Then where are they?" asked the Tubanters, because they could not see anything.

The stranger shook his head and went home. There he told his wife: "The Tubanters are good people, but they can't make jokes, oh no, they don't understand the first thing about it."

Now there also lived in that country a smith named Alec, a quiet and decent man, like all the rest. When this smith set up his own smithy through sheer hard work, he married a wife called Jennie and every evening they prayed for a son, whom they would call Hughie. And Hughie arrived one sunny day in April, just when the first lambs were frisking in the meadow. As soon as he was born he began to crow, until the sound filled the house.

"Alec!" cried his wife. "Come and see!"

"Has he come?" murmured the smith gravely. "I was just thinking, what's this I hear?" And he laid down his hammer and tongs and went to look.

It was a little boy, with red cheeks and bright blue eyes, just what they had always wished for. But what *was* the child doing!

"Wife!" cried the smith, aghast. "The boy is *laughing!* He's lying there, laughing! I know for sure, because that is just what the stranger did!"

"This is very serious," said the mayor, who had called for an official look, "very serious. If I were you—but of course you must do what you think best—if I were you I think I would fetch the sacristan."

The sacristan! That was a good idea. He knew everything, and a little bit more besides.

The sacristan came, put on his glasses and looked under them at the child.

"That is strange," he said gravely. "If I were you—well, I should apply some warm lettuce."

His mother did so, but at once the child began to laugh so heartily that everyone near burst out laughing, however solemn he had intended to be.

Then they fetched the parish priest. He was a wise man!

"I shall come," he announced, "with holy water and a brush. And if it be Satan himself, he will not prevail!"

The priest came, sprinkled the holy water over the child and pronounced a long prayer. But the little boy began to laugh, snatched the brush and splashed the drops of water to right and left.

"I'm being made a fool of," said the priest, "this is not the Evil One. It's simply a dratted boy!"

His words were well received.

"Oh, that Hughie!" people said, when they passed by his house and heard the ringing laughter. "He'll be all right. He's simply a dratted boy! Later on he will become a serious man like ourselves."

But that was just what did not happen. The older Hughie grew, the more cheerful and carefree he became. He did nothing but laugh, tell jokes and jump about. Yes, it was remarkable!

"Listen to me," said the smith one day, "this can't go on, you are almost a man now. You must be serious and learn a trade."

"Is that so," said Hughie, laughing, "all right, father."

"What do you want to be?" the smith asked him.

"It doesn't matter to me," said Hughie, laughing, "as long as it's something cheerful."

"Well, be a smith then," his father suggested. "I don't know if it's cheerful, but you have to do something."

"Everything is cheerful," laughed Hughie, picking up the hammer and striking the anvil until the sparks flew. So he became a smith, and what a smith! When he was hammering the shoes on the horses' hooves, he laughed so loudly that the poor creatures, unaccustomed to the noise, tore themselves loose and ran away. "Look at them running!" cried Hughie, and he burst out laughing. He sang and whistled all day long, one song after another, mingled with the silliest jokes and sayings.

Meanwhile those Tubanters who came from distant parts stood with their noses pressed to the windows of the smithy, gazing in at the

man who did such strange things with his mouth and made such extraordinary noises.

"How solemn you all look!" Hughie would laugh. "Why don't you
laugh too?"

"This life is a vale of tears, Hughie," the people called through the
window. "You will find that out soon enough."

"Is that so," said Hughie, "I didn't know."

"We are all miserable men and doomed to suffer on this earth,"
said a fat man.

"Is that so," said Hughie, "truly, I did not know."

"And then," another put in, "we must earn our bread in toil and
sweat."

"Is that so," said Hughie, "I didn't know that." And he began to
laugh.

"Why are you laughing now, Hughie?" asked the people.

"I can't help it," said Hughie, "I have to. I find the world so
beautiful."

This came to the ears of a minister. He flew into a passion and
stepped out of his carriage.

"I have heard about you, Hughie," he said, raising his finger. "For
shame, is this the way for a Christian to behave? Vengeance is the Lord's!
His eyes are like coals of fire and justice is in His Hand."

"Is that so," said Hughie, "I'll be sure to remember that. It sounds
so nice."

No, there was no talking to him.

"Now listen, Hughie," said his father, "here are two sandwiches for
you. Off you go."

"Thank you, father," said Hughie happily, "thank you very much.
I see there is jam in them. Goodbye."

"Get out!" cried the smith furiously, seizing his hammer and throwing it after him.

"Thank you, father," said Hughie, stooping, "what a splendid
hammer."

Then the smith flew into such a rage that he gave his son a kick
which sent him flying some way down the road. Hughie got up laughing
and said: "There, I shan't have to walk that bit now." Then he set off
into the wide world.

Stip-stap went his feet, it was a sunny day and Hughie was happier
than ever. Then he met the bishop. The bishop said: "Good morning,
happy Hughie, where are you off to now?"

"I don't know yet," said Hughie, "what should I do? The sun is in
the south, so I think I'll go south."

"Blessed are the poor in spirit," said the bishop, "but you know, Hughie, this evening it will be in the west."

"Then I will go west," said Hughie.

"Happy are the simple of heart," announced the bishop, "but then you will be going around in a big circle."

"Is that so," said Hughie, "one is always learning something new."

And so he walked around the country in a great circle, singing and skipping from one foot to the other.

"What are you going to *do*, Hughie?" the people called after him. For the Tubanters were always doing something.

"Do?" said Hughie, "Be happy, of course!"

"Hughie," others called, "where are you going?" Because the Tubanters were always going somewhere.

"I'm following the sun," said Hughie briskly. And on he went.

At last he came to a great city where there was a lovely smell of gingerbread. "I'm hungry," said Hughie to himself, "so let's find out where the gingerbread is, so that we can steal it." And he searched until he found the gingerbread in a shop.

"What a pity," said Hughie, "there's glass around it. So I shall have to break it." And he raised his hammer, smashed the glass to pieces and took the gingerbread.

Just then the judge passed by.

"Here, Hughie!" cried the judge. "What are you doing there?"

"I am stealing!" cried Hughie, laughing. "Can't you see that?"

When the judge heard this he put on his wig and said:

"This is very serious, Hughie. This is a solemn moment in your life."

"Is that so," said Hughie, "I didn't know."

"I believe that you will be put to death," announced the judge solemnly, "yes, Hughie, now I know for certain that you will lose your head."

"Then I'll have plenty left," said Hughie, following the judge to the courtroom.

There the high judge and his helpers settled down in cap and gown and looked sternly at Hughie.

"I've heard of you, Hughie," said the high judge, shaking his head, "you absolutely refuse to be serious. You follow the sun, pull all the young girls' braids and then you smash a window. You have made a fool of the bishop, the priest, the minister, the sacristan and even the judge. You make a fool of everyone. You seem to think life is something amusing."

"I do, your Worship," said Hughie.

"This is a fine thing," said the high judge, "where will it end? I had expected you here long ago. Now tell me you're sorry, at once."

"No, your Worship," said Hughie, "I'm not at all sorry for my life. It was terrific!"

"Right," said the high judge. "Then you must die."

"Then you must die," said all the other judges, when they heard this. And they looked as if they had thought it out for themselves.

"Die? Won't I be able to laugh any more then?" asked Happy Hughie.

"No," said the high judge, "you won't be able to laugh any more then."

"I don't believe that," said Hughie, laughing. "You can't kill happiness."

"Can't you just!" said the high judge angrily. "That's what you think! Executioner, do your duty!"

And the executioner led Hughie to the market place, where a great scaffold was standing.

"Look at the people!" cried Happy Hughie, when he was standing on the scaffold. "What a crowd! And I certainly have the best position in the whole market!"

"Come on, Hughie," said the executioner, "be serious for a moment. Lay your head on the block."

"I can't be serious," laughed Hughie, "but as to putting my head on the block, that is easy."

And he laid his head on the block and cried: "Go!"

Boom! His head rolled across the platform and stopped just at the edge, its face turned towards the people.

"Hello, people!" cried the head, laughing, "What do you think of this?"

Well, what did the people think? They took to their heels, tumbling over one another, and in a flash the square was empty.

"Ho, ho!" cried the head. "Where are you all going? Now listen to me! I know some really good ones!" And the head raised its voice until it echoed throughout the city; in fact the people heard his loud jokes and his hearty laughter deep in their cellars. It was terrible!

"You can't put happiness to death!" cried the judge. "He said it himself! There you are!" And he ran to see the king.

"King!" he said. "We have beheaded Hughie."

"Well, well," muttered the king, who was busy with something else at that moment, "beheaded. Imagine."

"Yes, but sire," cried the judge, "the head goes on laughing!"

"What's that you say?" cried the king. "What are you saying?"

The judge told him all.

"That is quite awful, judge," said the king at last, "but do you know what? You must sew the head in a sack and put it up in my attic. No one goes there."

"As you say, king," said the judge.

So the head was put in a sack and brought to the king's attic. But oh dear, the head laughed so loudly there that you could hear it all over the palace. People stopped in the street to stare up because they could see the glass quivering in the attic window panes.

"Oh dear, oh dear," sighed the king, stopping his ears, "this is terrible. If only we had not started all this. You can't get away from happiness! Now you see the result!"

So the judge was beheaded and the high judge too, and even the baker from whom the gingerbread had been stolen, although he had nothing to do with it. But the head laughed harder than ever, told a thousand jokes, and no one dared go up to the attic to bring it down. In the end the good king had to do it himself. He went tottering up the attic stairs with a velvet bag and approached the roaring head. It lay in a corner beside the bag because it had burst out from sheer merriment!

"Good morning, king!" said the head. "How nice of you to come and see me! I was just thinking that it was a little bit lonely up here!"

"Oh Hughie!" said the king. "Do stop! Can't you be serious for a moment? It's terrible, you're getting the whole country all mixed up. Oh, do be quiet now!"

"I have tried it from time to time," said the head, "but it's no use. I just have to be happy. There's nothing for it, I have to laugh for the lot of you. But the joke I'm going to tell you now will surely make you—"

"No!" cried the king resolutely. "You're going into the bag." And he shut his eyes tightly, grasped the head by the hair and stuffed it into the bag. But what then?

"Throw it in the lake, sire," said the chancellor. "It will sink!"

"Happiness doesn't sink!" said the head from the bag.

"We'll see about that!" cried the king angrily. And he whirled the bag around his head and threw it into the lake. But the head did not sink; it drifted slowly past some houses, laughing until the gables rang.

"The head! The head!" cried the people. "Oh, good king, take that dreadful head away and throw it in the well. We hear nothing but laughter and jokes all day long! It's not to be borne by serious people!"

"Will anyone take the head away?" the king called through the streets. "Eighty ducats for the man who does it, and perhaps even more."

Happy Hughie's own mother heard this.

"I'm not afraid of my own son," she said. "I'll get the head out of the water and throw it in the well. Then it will be at peace."

His mother stood at the water's edge.

"Hughie!" she cried. "You must be quiet. Be quiet now, son."

"I can't, mother!" the head called from the bag. "I have to laugh and be happy. I can't do otherwise!"

Then his mother wept and took the head out of the water, kissed its wet mouth and threw it in the well.

"Sand!" cried the king. "Sand!"

Judges, schoolmasters, greengrocers and even the bishop himself helped to fill in the well. And the ministers put their ears to the ground and listened.

"We can still hear something," they said. "Sand!"

"Sand!" cried the king.

At last they could hear nothing more, nothing at all. There was silence.

"Now Happie Hughie has gone," said the people, "and we can go home."

But listen to the wonderful end of this story. For in the very place where the head lay buried, a strange plant began to grow, a plant with long stems and red berries, for which there was no name. And when the first lambs began to frolic in the meadows, its little buds opened and its white flowers bloomed.

"Lovely!" thought a shepherd, who was passing with his sheep. Suddenly a smile spread over his solemn face and he picked a flower and bowed his head over its golden heart.

"I feel so happy," he said, "all my troubles have vanished! What a wonderful scent!"

He laughed, he actually laughed! And he gave the flower to his wife and she too laughed. And everyone who smelled the flower began to laugh, and forgot their troubles for a moment.

"We shall have to call it Laughwort," said the king. "That is my order!"

"Yes, *herbus risus!*" cried the scholars. "That's a good name!"

"Is it the same thing?" asked the king suspiciously.

"Exactly the same!" said the scholars.

"Then that's what we'll do," said the king.

And that's what they have done, right up to the present day.

And that is the story of Happy Hughie, or how the Laughwort began.

Fare you well.

The Four Wizards

ONCE upon a time there was a wicked wizard who lived among the rocks on a mountainside. At the foot of the mountain was a town where people lived. The people were very frightened of the wizard. When the weather was dry and the crops were shrivelling up in the fields he held back the rain clouds; and when it rained so hard that everything was under water, he gave a shrill cackle of laughter, released the clouds he had been saving up and clapped his hands with glee, for then even the houses were carried away by the flood. The mayor of the town had been to see him three times. He was always welcomed kindly. The wizard would offer him a cigar and say:

"Sit down. What can I do for you?"

"Oh," said the mayor, "you know very well."

"Why have you come?"

"To tell you again."

"Well, well," said the wizard. "Tell me, then."

And the mayor told him that another five pigs had been drowned and twelve families had no roof over their heads.

"You will have to start a disaster fund," said the wizard.

"We've done that," said the mayor eagerly, "but the people are poor and the fund is small."

The wizard laid a dollar on the table and the mayor put it gladly in his pocket, for every little bit helps.

"You have a good heart, really," he said.

"It is a great burden to me," said the wizard, "for my father was very different. Don't imagine *he* would have given you a dollar."

"Is your father still alive?"

"Yes. I learned a great deal from him. He does not make spells any more. He is resting. But a silver dollar? Never! I can just see him!"

"Where does your father live?"

The wizard stretched himself, for talking to a good man was already beginning to bore him.

"On the next mountain," he said, yawning. "Have a good trip."

The mayor scrambled over to the next mountain, and there he found an old wizard, whose hair was already grizzled, smoking a pipe at the opening of the cave where he lived. On the table inside stood two cups of tea. The mayor looked at them in astonishment.

"Did you know I was coming?"

"Yes, how could I help knowing? I already knew yesterday at half-past two. You have been to see my son, haven't you?"

"He really has a good heart," said the mayor.

The old wizard laughed grimly.

"A dollar," he said, "for the disaster fund. If only my old father could hear that. The world is getting better and better. There is nothing to be done any more."

"Is your father still alive?"

The old wizard cast his eyes upward.

"Is my father still alive?" he repeated bitterly. "Just be thankful he can't hear you. There is no killing him off. Do you take sugar and milk?"

"You really have a good heart," said the mayor. "Hospitality is quite unnecessary, and yet you are giving me tea."

The old man looked down gloomily.

"We all have our weaknesses," he said. "One fights them, of course, but sometimes they are too strong. And then one has to start again from the beginning."

"Where does your father live?" asked the mayor.

The old wizard shook so that the tears sprang into his eyes.

"A dollar," he said, "and for the disaster fund, of all things. Next mountain. You can't miss it."

The third wizard was so old that he no longer celebrated his birthday and had turned the calendar back to front. He said nothing when the mayor stood before him, for it did not matter to him at all. He just shook his head.

"Tea," he said, "with sugar and milk! Can you wonder that I sometimes lose heart?"

"Come now," said the mayor. "Head up!"

"Yes, yes, it's easy for you to talk," said the old man, "you have children who obey you. But when *I* have them, then where are we? 'Would you like some tea?' I can hear him saying it. He started early. And then it's not so easy to beat it out of them any more."

"Did you beat him much?" asked the mayor, who was beginning to understand.

"Not *much*, exactly," said the old man pensively, "but very hard. I had an iron rod with copper spikes. Every time he did a good deed I hit him. One does what one can. And *still* I was too weak."

"Your grandson is even worse than his father," said the mayor, who was seeing more and more.

"I don't want to talk about that boy," said the old man dismally. "He gave you a dollar, didn't he? Listen—when your own flesh and blood support the disaster fund, then it is time to give up."

"It's a shame," said the mayor excitedly, for he was beginning to get angry himself.

"If it had been a penny," resumed the old man, "I could understand. We're not all perfect."

"Not a halfpenny!" interrupted the mayor. "A father must be strict."

"Oh," said the ancient doubtfully, "we're only young once. Let us say a half-dollar."

"Out of the question! You must be tough, it is the only way."

"That was what my father always said," said the wizard regretfully. "If only I had listened to him!"

"Does he live hereabouts?" asked the mayor, for he suddenly felt a violent desire to meet the very toughest of them all.

"Next mountain," said the old man. "He is as hard as flint. But he is the very last."

The last wizard sat on a stone and looked fixedly at the mayor with his cold eyes.

"You have noticed," was all he said.

"Of course," said the mayor crossly, "you get weaker the farther down you come. But it's perfectly all right up here. At least, I hope so."

"Think it out," was all the wizard said.

"Now, take the potatoes," resumed the mayor. "Ours are good. But do you think it will hail?"

"Forget it," said the old man.

"And look at the wheat! Beautifully dry. And not a sign of rain."

"Just as I thought."

"And if we don't watch out, there will be a wonderful fruit harvest. The cherries are splendid."

"What do you expect?" said the old man bitterly. "*I* set the example."

"The water is not poisoned, either," the mayor went on angrily, "and we haven't had a blizzard for months."

The wizard suddenly sat up straight.

"Look here," he said, "you're not supposed to find it pleasant."

The mayor was not listening to him. "The strawberries," he said indignantly, "just melt on your tongue."

The old man peered at him in surprise.

"You are one of us," he said, "but that was not the idea!"

"And it is already three weeks," went on the mayor, "since I started the disaster fund. Where does the time go?"

The wizard jumped up and rushed over to the other mountain tops.

"Stop, boys!" he shouted while he was still far away. "They seem to enjoy it, and that means it's no more fun for us!"

So peace and well-being returned to the town at the foot of the four mountains. The water was drinkable and all the taps were in working order again. Only the mayor was not in working order. He was completely bewildered.

The Return

ONCE upon a time there lived a very rich man. He possessed everything a man could think of, and more besides, but he was not happy.

Once, when boredom was plaguing him even more than usual, he hit on the idea of making a journey. He had the horses harnessed and drove away. He drove all day at full gallop and towards evening he was rattling along the streets of an old town. The rich man woke up and looked attentively about him.

"Friend," he said to the coachman, "stop here for a minute. Something is bothering me."

The rich man sat up and looked thoughtfully at the gables of the houses. The bells were ringing and the scent of honeysuckle came wafting from the walled gardens. In the distance water was splashing in the fountains.

"All this," said the rich man, while a strange feeling overwhelmed his heart, "I have heard before. I have seen these gables before and I remember these sounds. I recall too the scent wafting from the gardens. But when can it have been?" He got out and told the coachman to return alone while he himself walked through the streets of the town, and his heart felt more and more strange.

In the end he stopped, fascinated, in front of an old house. It stood there in all gravity and yet the windows shone with a quiet and cheerful radiance in the moonlight. The rich man began to cry, because he remembered the house where he had lived as a child.

He was seen by an old priest who was passing the last years of his life behind one window of this house. He was a good-hearted man and he felt moved. He went outside, laid his hand on the stranger's shoulder and said:

"You are troubled. Tell me your sorrow so that I can help you."

"It is not sorrow," said the rich man. "It is joy, because I have found what I thought lost: the happiness of my childhood. Sell me the house. I will pay you anything you ask."

The priest thought for a minute. Then he smiled and said:

"I can be happy elsewhere, because happiness is not in the house but in the heart. Move in. Do what you like with it. I ask but one thing of you: Leave the saying which I have fixed above my bed where it is. It took me a whole lifetime to see the truth of it."

The rich man promised and moved into the old house. The first thing he saw was the saying above the bed. It said: "Happiness is within." The rich man could not restrain a smile. He wandered through the attics where he had played as a child and strolled down to the cellar where once, long ago, he had been shut in. He walked down the corridor where he ran as a boy and in his thoughts he heard his clear voice shouting. He entered the room where his father had worked and saw his grey head bowed over a desk and the light playing on his hair. He also visited the corner where his mother used to sit in the evening when she was tired from her worries, and the worn place in the floor where she used to put her feet. He saw all this as the tears filled his eyes. Next morning he walked in the garden and found the birds twittering in the ivy as of old. He sat under the may tree where he had sat as a little boy and picked up the white petals he had played with as a child. And by the third day he was bored.

"How's it going?" asked the old priest, visiting him one day.

"Reasonably," said the rich man, "but it is not as it used to be. I miss my father's servant who used to open the door when the bell rang and the nurse who punished me when my hands got dirty."

"That's easily attended to," said the old priest. "Both of them are still alive and live not far from here. I will fetch them. Wait a bit."

So both the old people moved to the house where they had lived in service when they were young. They rejoiced to see him and obeyed him.

"How's it going now?" asked the old priest, calling again after some time.

"Reasonably," said the rich man, "but it's not as it was. Everything has grown much smaller. Years ago I had to stand on my toes to reach the doorknob. I had to stretch up to look out of the windows at the garden. I can even remember being helped up when I tried to climb on a chair."

"That's easily attended to," said the old priest. "Have the house and everything in it rebuilt twice as large. You are rich enough, aren't you?"

That really is an excellent idea," said the rich man. "It shall be carried out this very day."

So the house was torn down and rebuilt twice as big. The windows were twice as high and even the chairs were twice as large as before.

Now the rich man had to stretch if he wanted to look out of the window at the garden and he was helped up when he took his seat at the table. The paintings were repainted twice the size as well, and even the saying over the bed was washed out and rewritten in giant letters. The biggest trees were planted in the garden and the coarsest gravel to be found was strewn on the path. The old priest could no longer look over the fence to ask how things were going, so he came in through the door.

"How's it going?" he asked, "is everything to your taste?"

"Reasonably," said the rich man, tossing a pebble in his hand, "and yet it is not as it was. The servant and the nurse have grown too small. I used to come up to their waists. And now they have to lift each other up to reach the door knob. It was different before. It worries me."

"That is easily attended to," said the old priest. "There is a circus not far from this town where you can see two giants, a man and a woman. Shall I send for them? You are rich enough, after all."

"Send them here at once," said the rich man, "that's the only thing I lack."

The two giants came. They were a man and a woman and they stood head and shoulders above him. They helped him to step over the threshold and lifted him into his chair when he wanted to sit down. On the second day after their arrival he was bored. But the old priest no longer came to ask him how things were going. So the rich man went to him and found him reading his Bible.

"What are you reading?" asked the rich man.

"I am reading," said the old priest, resting his wrinkled index finger on the page, "that unless you become as little children, you cannot enter the Kingdom of Heaven."

"And yet," said the rich man bitterly, "I have done all I could to reach heaven."

"You have done nothing," said the old man. "You have simply enlarged your surroundings. But you yourself must grow small. Happiness is not outside us. Happiness lies here, within. I had already written it over your bed, and one day I would like to be able to write it, truthfully, over your grave."

The Wind Man

HIGH above the clouds flew the wild wind man. His hair blew about his face, his eyes twinkled like stars and he laughed aloud. For the wind man enjoyed life. Over his shoulder he carried a sack and in it were all the winds.

There was the fresh west wind which always wanted to get out, for he was a merry youth and loved to romp. But he could do nothing about it; he had to wait until the wind man pulled him out by his curls.

There was the chill north wind, who always felt cold and crouched shivering in a corner. It was warm in the sack and he did not want to leave it. But there was nothing he could do either, for the wind man would seize him by his snow-white hair and, with a laugh, would fling him into the wide heavens.

And there was the east wind, who did not care what happened to him and would have preferred to be left in peace. But it was all right with him when the wind man took him by his black hair and threw him into the air. Then he stretched out to his full length and began to blow. His sombre eyes glowed and his icy fist reached out over the earth.

Then there was the gentle south wind. She was the only woman among them and this was a little difficult for her, as you will understand, but she kept her kindly nature. And when the wind man took her by her fair tresses she stood up of her own accord, unfolded her wings and rose slowly into the blue sky. And a balmy wind blew over the frozen earth, and ice began to melt and flowers bloomed amidst the grass as far as the eye could see. All these the wind man carried with him and that was why he enjoyed life.

But today he was in a specially good mood. He had just let out the south wind and now he was flying high above the green meadows and the waving tree-tops. He could see the windmills turning along the shining rivers and the people, small as dolls, working in the fields.

"But I would like to hear if they are happy," thought the wind man and for the first time in his life he folded his wings and plunged towards the earth. He found a farmer's smock and put it on, hiding his wings under it so that no one would know he was the wind man. Then he went into an inn. It was full of farmers, who looked tired and hot.

"There is a draft here," said one of them. "Where did that sudden cold wind come from?"

The wind man stooped under the table where his sack was lying and saw the sombre eyes of the east wind glowing through a gap.

"Inside, you!" he whispered. "It is not your time yet. And now, good people, are you content with the weather?"

"Oh, no," said the farmers, "it is much too warm. The crops are drying up in the fields. Pray God the rain comes, otherwise we are all lost."

The wind man started. "Your prayers will be heard," he said solemnly.

He went out, unfolded his wings and released the west wind into the sky. At once the clouds gathered and the rain poured down onto the parched earth. And once again the wind man dived down and asked the people if they were content.

"Oh, no," said the people. "We have worked all week in order to go out on Sunday. And see how it is raining. God grant that it clears up, for otherwise our day is ruined."

And the wind man was taken aback. "Your prayers will be heard," he said solemnly.

Again he unfolded his wings and the rain stopped. And because he did not know what would satisfy the people he kept all his servants in his sack and the day was still and not a leaf stirred. And again the wind man plunged earthwards and met a miller. He asked him if he was content.

"Oh no," said the miller, "the sails stand still all day. If no wind comes my wife and children will starve."

The wind man was horrified.

"What wind would you like?" he asked.

"God grant that it is an east wind," replied the miller, "for that is the strongest."

"Your prayers will also be heard," said the wind man solemnly, "although I am beginning to doubt if I am doing any good."

And he rose into the sky on his broad wings and at once a great storm rushed in from the east. And when the wind man saw all the sails of the windmills turning he suddenly felt cheerful again. He swooped hopefully down and expected to see only happy faces.

But the first person he met was a weeping woman.

"God save my husband and son at sea," she moaned, "for if this goes on, they will be lost, lock, stock and barrel."

The wind man was horrified.

"Your prayers will be heard," he said solemnly, "for the water will turn to ice."

And high above the driving clouds he released the north wind. At once the water froze and the world was covered with snow. But the people suffered hunger and cold and there was not one who rejoiced.

Then the wind man recalled the north wind and began to fly all alone. He flapped silently over the frozen world and tears welled from his eyes. And they fell upon the earth and the beating of his wings stirred only the tops of the trees. So the wind man flew across the earth. And the earth recovered and gradually began to flower.

"What is that?" a child asked.

"May-time rain," said his mother, "and that means it is spring. And do you feel the balmy wind? It is as if an angel were passing by."

And they both stretched out their hands and felt the May rain on their faces and were happy. And everywhere people drew a breath of relief and rejoiced.

But the wind man did not know it. He flew on alone and tears of grief ran down his face. He cried because he could not bring happiness. Yet he brought it wherever he went.

Anita

ANITA Gamblepat has just been born, in a great, crimson rose. She stretches her wings until they are smooth, saying: "There, here I am! What a splendid view there is from here! Splendid! Splendid!"

"You mustn't shout like that, child," said Mrs. Gamblepat, "and you mustn't fidget, either."

Readers must understand just who Mrs. Gamblepat was. You might easily look upon her as an ordinary maybug, and you would be quite wrong. Her father was a member of the Council and her husband was secretary of the Maybugs' Union, "Strength Through Unity." If that isn't worth a ribbon, as the mayor once said, the wasps can come and get me. But he got his ribbon. And he got another one, and another, and then another. In the end he had so many medals that he jangled horribly as he flew and he could only stay in the air for quite a short time.

"But," said Mr. Gamblepat, "every rose has its thorn." And he limited his outings according to his range. I am telling you all this so that you may know who Mrs. Gamblepat was and why she did not like to have any fidgeting or shouting. But although *we* know this, a small maybug who has just been born, in a great crimson rose, does not know it.

"Why can't I shout?" she asked. "And why can't I fidget?"

"A Gamblepat does not shout," said her mother. "A Gamblepat does not fidget. And that is precisely what makes us different from our neighbors. Look, here comes your father."

And there indeed was Mr. Gamblepat, flying towards them. He was jingling like a horse-sled when he settled, panting, on the edge of the flower.

"Well, well," he said, "so that's flying. Every rose has its thorn. Yes. What's that?"

83

"That is your child, John," replied Mrs. Gamblepat, bursting into tears. "I thought you would take more interest in household events than that."

"There, there," said Mr. Gamblepat, wiping his brow and looking about him in some embarrassment, "I had quite forgotten. After all, we get one every month. Don't cry, Joanna, I can't bear that. M'm, it's a nice little girl. What's your name?"

"Anita Gamblepat," said little Anita proudly.

"Ah," said Mr. Gamblepat, "welcome to our midst. Is there any tea?"

There was some tea. If some passer-by had seen them sitting in the red cup of the flower, each on one of the three stamens, rocking in the wind and delicately sipping dew from their costly tea service, he would have said: what a happy family! But it was not so. Mr. Gamblepat was thinking about the rose in which the Nettleman family lived. That had four stamens.

"Four," thought Mr. Gamblepat bitterly, swallowing his tea down, "four. And we have three. I wish I had never been born."

Mrs. Gamblepat was unhappy too. She was thinking of the tea service from which the Nettlemans were drinking. Once, when it was Mrs. Gamblepat's birthday, Mrs. Nettleman had held one of her own cups up to the light. The sun shone right through it, it was so fine.

"You can't get them any more," she had said.

"Why her?" thought Mrs. Gamblepat, stirring her cup to see if there was any sugar left in the bottom. "Why not us? I wish I was dead."

That was what they thought, and they did not notice that the sun shone through the walls of their own little house and that the room in which they were sitting so unhappily was more fragile than glass. Even little Anita was unhappy, but she herself did not know why. A great longing was welling up in her heart, she longed to fidget and shout, but a Gamblepat doesn't fidget and a Gamblepat doesn't shout.

Evening fell quickly over the red blossom and it closed. The lamp was put out. Little Anita sat on her father's knee, playing with all his medals.

"What are these, father?" she asked.

Her father smiled.

"Ha, ha," he said, "the five before you all asked the same question. Those are medals, little one. Look, the one on the left, with the lion on it, that was because your dad spent two years on the school committee. And the one next to it is for something else. And the one next to that is for the Swampland Reclamation Committee—they all mean something."

"They jingle so prettily," said little Anita, patting them with her hand.

Mr. Gamblepat smiled at his wife and said: "She has no idea."

Anita Gamblepat was still very young. She wanted to know everything.

"Where is the sun, father?"

"Gone."

"And when will it come back?"

"Tomorrow."

"What will we do then?"

"Pay visits."

"And then?"

"Eat."

"And then?"

"Sleep."

"And then?"

"Then you will be a big girl and you will get married."

"Whom shall I marry?"

"Father and mother have chosen young Jinglefoot for you."

"But I don't want to marry young Jinglefoot!" cried little Anita excitedly, "I want to marry a nice, handsome boy with golden wings and silver wingsheaths and red feelers and we'll go and live in a scarlet poppy and we'll fidget about all day and jump in the sun and we'll shout too . . ."

"Anita Gamblepat must be sensible," said Mrs. Gamblepat, raising her eyebrows, "and not talk nonsense. Anita Gamblepat has a position to maintain and jumping about in the sun will do nothing to help. Do you think your father became a member of the Council by jumping about in the sun? And as for young Jinglefoot, whom Papa has selected for you, he has something more substantial than red feelers."

"What has he got, then?" asked Anita, with her nose to the wind.

"A position in the Government," said Mrs. Gamblepat slowly.

"What do I care about the gubbermint!" screamed little Anita, beating her wings. "I want to romp and fly and—" But she was picked up and tucked into bed, where she cried all night.

Next day visits were paid, food was eaten, sleep took place, and on the third day she was a fat shiny maybug and married young Jinglefoot, with his government position. They leased a vacant dandelion with central heating and a view of the meadow. And this very morning Anita

Gamblepat has had a baby, Anita Jinglefoot, who wants to fidget and shout.

But of course, a Jinglefoot doesn't shout and a Jinglefoot doesn't fidget.

And here the story begins all over again.

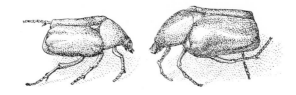

Frederica

ONCE upon a time there was a hen called Frederica. At the moment when this little tale begins she was sitting in the sunshine between the sand pit and the rosebush. It was a beautiful day. The sun stood high in the blue sky and it was so still that you could hear the distant traffic on the road.

This was the time that Frederica liked. She looked about the silent garden and murmured: "Now I am happy. Yes, I really do believe this is happiness. So still, so peaceful. And yet I can see everything that is going on in the world. I can see the rubber ball under the shed, the white post with the dovecote on it, the gnats dancing above the lettuces and even two aphids exchanging a first shy kiss on a crimson rose." Frederica smiled when she saw this. It made her think of her own young days and that first, wonderful evening when he had said: "May I — may I take a little walk with you?"

Frederica blushed as she remembered. How dear and courteous he had been, and what depths had glowed in his beady eye as he insisted that without her life for him was empty. His name was Jack. Then he had run off with another and Frederica could sit on her eggs. She stood up and counted them again. There were five—five prosperous eggs. She smiled proudly and sat down again, deep in thought.

What was life? Life was completely beyond understanding. And the more you thought about it, the more puzzling it became. Most incomprehensible of all was the life of a married woman. One morning, not long after her wedding, she had deposited a longish, smooth ball in the sand. Frederica had looked at it in surprise for some time and then sat on it. Next day she had another one, just as smooth and incomprehensible. And so five days had passed and now she had been sitting on her five eggs for just three weeks and was getting more surprised every day.

"Why am I sitting here?" she had asked Jack, when he walked by with his new love.

"But, dear child," Jack had said, "if you don't like it, get off!"

Frederica had tried this several times, but scarcely had she moved two steps when a sharp pang of conscience pierced her little heart. "No," she had said each time, "it may seem odd, but I am staying." And she had stayed, for three whole weeks, and now it was Tuesday. Frederica looked around the garden and felt in wonderful spirits. It seemed to her that something was going to happen, but she did not know what. She was just going to cackle when something moved beneath her.

"This must be it," said Frederica, and she stood up, trembling.

Then she saw the most incomprehensible thing of all: five downy little creatures jumped out of the white fragments into the world and went stumbling off through the lettuces. Frederica did not understand, but a deep joy filled her heart and without enquiring any further she went off eagerly to grub out worms and maybugs. The young man who was sliding cautiously down from a nearby apple tree did not quite understand, either. But he went indoors and wrote down this little story.

The Toys

ONCE upon a time there were two children, a sister and a brother, and they were lying in bed, crying. They had no father and no mother — at least, that was what they thought — and therefore they had been sent to live with an old aunt. She was not a real aunt, they knew that. She was an old witch. She beat the children by day with a broomstick and at night she crept downstairs in her slippers and licked the jam off their bread and butter. She drank their mugs of milk, too, and when the brother was playing one day with the top his father had given him long ago, the old woman said: "That is mine!" And she stuffed the top into her red petticoat.

That was when the two children realized that the old woman was a witch and that was why they were crying so bitterly this day. The moon shone in through the window of their attic room and they were terribly cold; it was freezing so hard that the timbers creaked.

"Listen," said the little girl. "Don't I hear the cracking of a whip?"

They ran to the window and down below in the garden they saw the old woman playing with the top. It was midnight, but because the moon was shining they could see her clearly as she stood there in her white nightdress. She cracked the whip until the top began to hum. Harder and harder she whipped, until at last the top began to sing. And this was what it sang:

> "She looks like a woman, but that she is not,
> Dear children, run now from this terrible spot!"

The little girl heard nothing, for it was not her top. But the boy to whom it had been given understood it plainly.

"We must run away at once," he said.

He took the kite, of which he was very fond because he had found it himself, and she took the doll she loved best and also the little silver mug her mother had once given her, long before. That was very long ago, when the children's parents were both still alive, but now they were dead. At least, that was what the poor children thought, but it was not true.

Together they crept out through the kitchen door. The top was still lying on the gravel path and the boy quickly put it in his bag. for he was very fond of the top. Then they looked about them. It was bitterly cold and they could not hear a single sound. The snow was falling in huge flakes, but the brother held the kite above their heads so that the wind caught and pulled it and they ran hand in hand into the dark night.

At last they came to the shore of a great lake and they could go no farther, because the lake had not yet frozen over. But the boy put the kite on the water and they floated on it to the opposite bank. When they reached the opposite bank, the sun came up and it was day.

The two children looked about them, but there was no one to be seen. The little girl was frightened. She said:

"We are lost!"

But her brother replied: "That is not possible. You can only be lost when you are going somewhere. And we are not going anywhere."

The girl thought about this and realized that he was right. But she grew frightened again and said:

"We are quite alone."

Her brother answered: "That is not possible. You are alone when there is only one of you. And there are two of us."

The little girl thought about it, and once again said she realized that he was right. But then she said:

"I am hungry and there is nothing to eat."

Her brother did not know the answer to this one. He looked at the ground and began to cry.

"Both my toys have helped us," he said. "My top warned us and my kite carried us across the water. But what has your doll done for us?"

The little girl unwrapped the doll from her apron where she had kept it safely, and laid it on the ground. And at once the doll closed its blue eyes, for it could do that. The little girl made it sit up slowly and the doll opened its bright blue eyes, saying:

> "She flies on the wind so wild, my child,
> So hold the string tight, my little mite."

The brother heard nothing, for the doll was not his, but the sister heard the words clearly. And at once a great wind arose and in the distance they could see the old witch coming towards them on her broomstick. She was flying straight through the clouds and shaking her fist.

"Fly your kite!" cried the little girl, "and hold fast to the string!"

The boy flung his kite into the air and they held fast to the string. The kite flew more and more swiftly and they skimmed faster and faster over the ground. But faster still the old woman flew on her broomstick, and all the time they could hear her harsh laughter. Then the kite pulled them off the ground and rose through the clouds. The two children held fast and when they looked around they saw the broomstick shrinking back into the distance. The old woman gave a loud shriek. In her fury she lashed the wind to a great storm and then to a hurricane, but the harder the wind blew, the faster flew the kite before her. Then the old woman turned for home in a fury and went to sit on the floor of her cellar to think up some new tricks. The wind died and the world was still again.

The kite floated down with the two children into a great meadow where cows were grazing. The cows had just been milked, and buckets of milk stood on the grass. The little girl dipped her silver mug into one of the buckets. And for the first time in years the children drank milk again, for all that time the wicked witch had been drinking their mugs dry every night.

"Where there are cows there are people, too," said the brother, and they went to look for a house where people lived. But they did not find one, because a white mist magically rose from the grass. The children walked round and round in their search — and now they were *really* lost: that was the old woman's new trick. Back in her cellar, she clapped her hands gleefully and pulled on her magic slippers. They carried her faster than the wind and now she rushed across the ground like wildfire. The boy heard the crackle of her red petticoat in the distance and began to weep with terror. But the little girl put her doll on the grass. And at once it closed its blue eyes, for it could do that. The girl made it sit up slowly, and as the doll opened its eyes wide, it said:

> "Though the witch will not stop,
> Just follow the top."

The brother heard nothing, because the doll was not his. But the little girl to whom the doll had been given understood the words clearly.

"You must spin the top," she said, "then we shall find the people."

So the boy took the top and flung it on the grass. And the top began to spin, faster and faster until at last it was whirling so fast that it bored

a hole in the ground and disappeared. The children took each other by the hand and went down the hole into the dark earth. The top sang and hummed before them and this is what it sang:

> "I know what you want and I know your plight,
> So follow my trail through the darkest night."

The little girl could not hear it, for the top was not hers, but the boy had understood. He realized that something extraordinary was going to happen and he pulled his sister forward impatiently. And at last they reached a cellar. Here the top began to turn more slowly and in the end it stopped and fell over on its side. There they were, standing in the dark, unable to see their hands before their eyes, and the little girl was so frightened that she dropped her mug. As the silver object clattered on the stone floor, the walls echoed the sound.

The noise was heard by two people who were sitting in the room above the cellar. They were terribly sad, for long ago when their two children were still very small, an old witch had come and said to them:

"You are too poor to feed your children properly. Give them to me. I will give them bed and board."

She had said it with a strange laugh, but the good parents suspected nothing and bravely gave up their children because they loved them dearly and could not bear to see them go hungry. They had never heard of them again, so they thought that their children were dead, and every evening they wept as they sat at the table, one on each side. The children's two chairs stood empty against the wall and whenever they saw them the parents began to cry again. Suddenly the mother sat up straight and listened.

"I heard something falling," she said. "It is our daughter's little mug."

"And I heard a top humming," said the father. "It is the top that I gave our son."

And they ran, helter-skelter, to open the cellar door. There stood their two children! Oh, how happy they were! They flew into one another's arms and the mother went at once to bake ginger cakes, which she always did on their birthday. And the father filled his pipe, which he was not usually allowed to do because it made the curtains black. And he carefully put away the top, the kite, the mug and the doll in a cabinet, locked the door and hung the key on a nail.

"We must take care of those toys," he said, "for they have made all four of us happy."

And so it was. No one ever opened the cabinet, but they could look in through the glass panels and see the toys. And when the children grew up and had children themselves, they told them the story of the toys, and they too saw with their own eyes that it had really happened.

The witch? Well, she knew it was all over. She walked all round the house once more and peered through the windows. When she saw the children eating gingerbread, the father smoking a pipe and the mother glancing at the curtains with a smile, she gave a shriek and flew through the clouds, straight towards the south. Folk saw her red petticoat over London, over Paris and over Madrid, which is the capital of Spain. And after that nothing was ever seen of her again.

The Curse

ONCE upon a time a curate was walking through the town, deep in holy thoughts. Coming to a street corner, he bumped right into an Italian chimney sweep and they rolled on the ground together. The chimney sweep shook his fist at the priest, uttered a mighty curse, turned his back and went on his way.

But the curate stayed sitting on the cobbles where he was. He looked at his round hat, which lay a little way off, and suddenly he knew, with the certainty which comes only through fasting and mortification, that the curse was imprisoned under his large hat And since he was not only an inwardly spiritual man but also capable of great energy outwardly, he jumped up, clamped the hat firmly against his body and ran to the presbytery

"I've got him!" he cried breathlessly.

"*Deo gratias,*" said the priest, "make sure you hold on to him and don't let him escape again. Did a lot of iniquities come out?"

"This is the biggest sinner I have every caught," said the curate, "and he is inside my round hat."

"Sinners who can be caught under a hat," remarked the priest thoughtfully, "are rare. Just tell me calmly what happened."

The curate told his shepherd what had happened to him.

"I've got him here," he finished, burning with a divine fire, "but I'm going to kill him."

"Thou shalt not kill," said the priest, "and moreover, thou shalt forgive those that trespass against you. So shut him up in the offertory box."

The curate shook the curse out of his hat through the slit of the offertory box and secured it with three padlocks. It was a heavy little box, with the words "St. Peter's Penny" written on it. Even a curse would have found it impossible to get out.

For three days he cursed in a shrill voice and made vain attempts to squeeze through the slit. But when he was surrounded by more and more pious coins, he fell silent and relapsed into surly gloom. The curate was promoted to a parish and the priest died and forgot the curse entirely in eternal bliss. That is the characteristic of the Blessed, they forget the bad things and are filled with pure goodness. Even the curate forgot the event, because he was a simple and forgetful man. But the curse did not forget. Yet his outbursts of temper grew rarer and rarer and when at last a coin bearing the inscription "God Be With Us" fell on his head, he gave up hope.

After a year the little box was fetched by a silent man dressed in black, who poured the contents into a larger box which stood at the back of the church. And after another year a man came there to empty the contents into a great offertory chest which stood at the back of the cathedral. And after yet another year a man came there, too, to empty the five boxes of the five bishoprics into one gigantic copper chest belonging to the main cathedral. This chest was emptied only every two years. All that time the curse was lying there among the coins, big and small, gnashing his teeth.

When the two years were past the chest was put on a train and sent to Rome. There it was taken to the Vatican, where the Pope happened to be walking in the garden.

"Just put the chest there," said the Holy Father, "and summon all the poor of Rome."

The poor of Rome streamed into the Vatican garden and the Pope handed each of them a linen bag of money. The bag in which the curse was hidden was handed to a chimney sweep. And see how wonderful the ways of the world can be: it was the same chimney sweep who had once cursed the priest! And as soon as he received the bag he remembered his sin and told the Holy Father what he had done. The Pope considered for a minute.

"Go back to the place where it happened," he said at last, "and find the priest you offended against. He is sure to forgive you."

So the chimney sweep returned to that place and looked for the priest he had injured. He swept all the chimneys of all the presbyteries in all five bishoprics, and at last, after twenty years, he descended a narrow chimney and found himself facing an old priest reading his breviary in the lamplight. He recognized him at once.

"I've got him!" cried the chimney sweep.

"*Deo gratias,*" said the priest, "make sure you keep him. Did many iniquities come out?"

"As for that," said the chimney sweep, "it was the cleanest chimney I ever saw."

"They are rare in presbyteries," said the priest thoughtfully. "Just tell me calmly what you have really come for."

The chimney sweep told him what had happened. How he had cursed him, as a curate, and how he had been to the Pope and remembered his curse. How he had then searched through all the presbyteries of the country. Then the old priest recognized him too and tears came into his eyes. He told the sweep what had happened to him as well. How he had put the curse in the offertory box and then forgotten it, because he was a forgetful man. And how he had come back much later and found the box emptied.

"I forgive you readily," he said. "Here is my hand."

He gave the chimney sweep his hand and at the same moment a loud cry burst from the linen bag which lay between them. It was the curse, breathing his last. He had held out for twenty-five years among the consecrated coins, but this was too much for him and he laid his head on a cent and died.

"What was that?" asked the chimney sweep, alarmed.

But light dawned on the priest.

"I think," said he, "that that is our old curse in there. Good heavens, that would be a coincidence! It's like a fairy tale."

"If that is true," cried the chimney sweep, burning with a divine fire, "I will kill him!"

"Thou shalt not kill," said the priest, "and moreover thou shalt forgive those that trespass against you. So open the bag."

The bag was opened, and there was the curse. He was a fiery-red little man, quite naked and no bigger than a matchstick. He had stuffed his fingers in his ears, and he was as dead as a doornail.

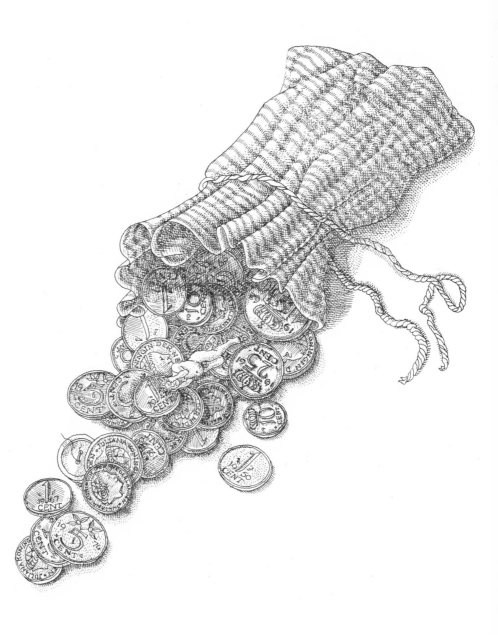

The
Echo
Well

ONCE upon a time there was a girl, who, to be honest, was not very beautiful. She had a hump on her back and her nose was rather crooked. And she stuttered dreadfully. Nevertheless, someone married her. Now, her husband was not handsome either. He had bow legs and he could not say his g's. Furthermore, he had a squint. But they were very happy together and both families turned up for the wedding.

What an extraordinary gathering that was! Half of them had crooked noses and the other half could not say their g's, so they amused one another greatly. When they had stopped laughing about this, the hunchbacks looked at the bandy legs, and the aunts with a squint listened to the uncles who stuttered, and the merriment began afresh. So each was delighted with himself and thought the others were oddities indeed. They gave the bridal couple all sorts of broken presents and when they had finished, the godfather of the bridegroom appeared. He was the only member of the family whose legs were straight and who could even say his g's. He gave presents that were all in one piece, too, and he was therefore regarded as an eccentric by the family. And so he was. For this is what he said:

"Children," he said, "at present life may seem all moonlight and roses, but there will come a time when you are in difficulties. I know the world, for my legs are straight and I have no trouble with my g's. And so I am going to give you a whistle. If poverty knocks at the door, blow on the whistle and everything will turn out all right."

Both families roared with laughter; they thought the whistle funny because nothing was wrong with it and the godfather himself they thought funny because he was sound in wind and limb.

Yet the man was right. Before a year had passed the young people were living in bitter poverty. They grew peevish and saw each other's faults. They did love one another, but you cannot live on love alone. And in the end it grew so bad that the husband could clearly see that his wife's nose was not straight and she could clearly hear that he could not say his g's.

"Th-this can't g-go on," muttered the wife, "for he will s-soon s-see that I have a h-hump, and where will our h-happiness b-be then?"

Now this was a very wise thought, for her intelligence was high. And so she remembered the little whistle. She hunted for a week among all the broken presents and at last she found it, in the place where she had put it so that it could be found at once. And she had hardly blown upon it when a dwarf appeared. He was a handsome little fellow and his legs were straight. The young couple gazed at him in astonishment.

"Here's a fine thin'," said the man, "we haven't even enough for two to eat and now this fellow will want feedin'! What strange le's he has. They do not even look crooked!"

"Look here," said the dwarf, "I'm as good as I was made."

"He can even say his g's!" cried the woman; "he is a strange p-person."

"When you have quite finished," said the dwarf, "will you be so good as to tell me what you called me for?"

"He doesn't even stutter," said the man, "and I can't see his hump either. Are you quite certain that it was the *right* whistle?"

"Look here," said the dwarf, "I know you well. I have been in this house for a whole year, for I belong to the whistle. I have been watching you and you are very good people. You admired each other's failings and that is the way to live a married life. And I should know, for I am married myself. We are both very small, but we do not notice it. We simply find other people rather large."

"My wife's nose is straight," said the man who could not say his g's.

"And my husband doesn't s-squint, either," said the wife who stuttered.

"Fine," said the gnome happily. "But that is not enough. You must not just *bear* with each other's failings, you must also *make* something of your faults. And that is why I am going to give you an echo well."

"What's that?" asked the man.

"I will show you," said the mannikin.

He ran out and stood by an old well at the end of the garden. There was a wild vine growing over it, and when you pushed this aside you could see a deep, dark hole. The well was so deep that no bucket had ever reached the bottom.

"Why do you not use it?" asked the gnome.

"It is m-much too deep," said the woman.

"That's just it," said the gnome. "The well is much too deep, but that is what is good about it. Now I will leave you here. Stay here for five minutes and talk to one another. You need do nothing more. I'm going to write a letter to the king."

And with that he vanished.

The husband and wife stayed by the well for five minutes as they had been told to do. She poked her crooked nose curiously over the edge and he also looked down with his squinting eyes. But they could see nothing, for the water was too deep. And as they stood there they talked about the dwarf. The visit had been so strange that the wife stuttered even more than before and the husband had such difficulties with his g's that he almost fell over the edge. And all this time the well was silent. They could hear a confused humming, but that grew weaker and weaker and nothing came back. They stayed there listening and then went back to the house, shaking their heads.

The next day the king called. He was surrounded by his whole court and his treasurer carried a sack of money on his back.

"Good people," he said, "I received a letter this morning. Apparently there is a well here and it talks about a dwarf. Very amusing. And it talks with a stammer, too, and that is even more amusing."

"Yes," said the queen, "and it can't say its g's."

"Quite," said the king, "and when you look down, you see a young woman with a hump back and a man with a squint."

"You've forgotten the crooked nose," said the queen, "and I think that's the funniest of all."

And when they looked down over the edge, everything was just as the letter had said. For the well was so deep that even the reflection had had to travel for a day and a night to reach the surface. The king slapped his knees with delight and the queen almost fell into the well with laughter. The king, too, had to cling tightly to the edge, for his own nose was straight.

"What fun," he said, drying his eyes with his embroidered handkerchief. "Phew, that did make me laugh! And it really does stutter. But the hump back is the best thing of all!"

"And don't forget the squint," said the queen.

"That is for connoisseurs," said the king, who happened to wear glasses. "Personally I liked the story very much, for I am mad about dwarfs. And now, good people, how much do you want for the well?"

And the wife, who stammered, meant to say: "All the gold in the world would not part us from it," but she got no further than the first few words: "All the gold in the world."

The king nodded. "Of course," he said, "I quite understand. And how much does that really mean?"

And the man who could not say his g's wanted to answer: "Go! I won't sell it for a thousand pounds," but he said: "Oh, I won't sell it for a thousand pounds," for that was the best he could do. The king clapped him on the shoulder.

"Quite right," he said affably, "one thousand is too little. Let's make it ten." And because he was the king no one could say no to that.

And that was a very good thing, for listen to what happened next: the well with the wild vine over it was moved to the palace and placed in the middle of the palace garden. But alas, after it was moved, it no longer stammered and it echoed its g's just like any other well. Say what he would, only the king's own words came back to him, and that is what kings hear all day long. Look as he would, he could see only himself, and that is just what kings always see. Poor king, truth really lived at the bottom of his well.

The two misshapen people lived on the ten thousand pounds until they died, for that is a great deal of money. But the little whistle disappeared and they never found it again.

Nothing

THE king was walking in his garden. It was the middle of May. The sun was shining, the fountains leaped sparkling into the air, and goldfish the size of dolphins shot through the glittering water. An orchestra was playing in the arbor and seven dancing girls were dancing through the rose gardens. Jugglers were juggling everywhere and a ventriloquist was performing on the center path. The king yawned.

"If only something would happen," he said. "This is quite deadly."

But he could not think of anything that ought to happen, because everything he could think of was already happening. Then he called his Minister of Pleasure and Entertainment and said:

"Please think of something new."

"Fireworks," said the minister.

The fireworks arrived. The rockets, arrows and fireballs shot into the air and finally the whole palace flew into the air with them.

"How boring," said the king, when it was all over. "Can't you think of something *nice?*"

"A circus," said the minister.

The circus arrived. There was a camel which played the flute and six elephants who did something which elephants do not usually do and there was a spotted beast which could say "Thank you." The king sat in the front row, yawning until the tears sprang into his eyes.

"Well, that's over now," he said when it was finished. "Can't you think of anything which made you say: now that is *really* funny?"

"Myself," said the minister. He took off his coat and went and stood on his head in the grass. Then he spun round like a mad thing, humming a song.

"Feeble," said the king, when he had finished. "I want to see some-

thing precious. A glass house, with diamond windows. And when it's finished, I shall smash it up with a stick."

A house was built. Everything, tables, chairs, pillows, beds and the coal in the cellar, was made of glass, and the diamond windows sparkled like diamonds. When it was ready the king ran through it, smashing it up with a stick. The splinters flew round his head and his ears were full of them. But when everything was broken and he wanted to think up a new idea the minister said:

"There's no money left."

"Then sell the palace," said the king.

"The palace has been blown up."

"The humming top again," said the king, "that was the best thing."

"Get it yourself," said the minister. And he went away.

Then the king realized that he was poor. He picked up his stick again and set out into the world. He met many people and asked them all for work and bread. But the people asked:

"What can you do?" And he replied: "Nothing. Nothing at all."

The people shrugged their shoulders and went on their way.

Now it happened one day that he came, tired and hungry, to a field where a man was lying on his back, gazing at the sky.

"What are you doing there?" asked the king curiously.

"Nothing," said the man, "nothing at all."

"Just so," said the king. "I have been doing that for twenty years."

"I do it for twenty minutes," said the man, "and even then I begin to get thoroughly bored."

He got up and began to reap the corn, and the king reaped with him. When it was evening they lay down among the sheaves and looked at the stars. This went on for several weeks. Then the king returned to his kingdom, his usefulness restored. He looked over the wall at the palace gardens and saw that there were now fourteen dancers dancing through the rose garden. There were spotted animals who not only said "Thank you," but also "Keep to the right" and "See you tomorrow," and the sun stood like a pale balloon between the explosions of the fireworks. A new king sat on his throne, looking on and yawning.

"Listen to me!" cried the former king. "Go and work! Work all day and rest in the evening. Then you will know what it is to do nothing for ten minutes. It is heaven on earth, the paradise of paradises!"

The new king lifted his head and yawned.

"Chase that tramp off," he said. "He bores me too."

The Misunderstanding

LONG ago there was an old man who lived in an old house. He still wore a short pigtail, although there was not another soul in the world who wore one, and a three-cornered hat which had long been out of fashion. He lived in a silent house whose tall windows overlooked the waters of a narrow, glassy moat which no one crossed any more. Behind the house was a large, walled garden, with never a child to wander singing down the paths. Only the old man entered it now and then, tapping his stick from time to time against the gnarled trunks of the fruit trees. Sometimes he picked an apple and took it indoors with him, where his old housekeeper cut it in half and put it in the oven. The housekeeper was even older than the old man and one day she died. When the old man returned from the cemetery and put his key in the front door, an extraordinary thought came to him.

"Death has forgotten me!" he said. "He has passed me by. A mistake has been made. All the members of my family, all my friends and everyone I have ever known have passed away and been buried. There has been a misunderstanding."

He closed the door quickly behind him and shot the bolt. The sound echoed through the empty house.

"I shall close the shutters at the windows," said the old man, "and I shall put out the fire in the hearth, so that there is no smoke to betray my presence."

He closed the shutters in front of the windows and put out the fire in the hearth, so that there was not smoke rising from the chimney to betray him. Then he walked around the old house, locking all the rooms, and bolted the trap-door to the cellar. He went into his silent courtyard and nailed up the little door through which people could enter. Back in his house, he turned the key of the kitchen door and dealt with all the traces which might indicate the presence of an inhabitant. Then he

went to sit in the smallest room of his house, which looked out onto his silent garden.

There he sat, motionless, looking at the dusk gathering outside the little window.

But after some time the old man felt hungry. He walked through the house looking for bread, but he found nothing, and he realized that he had made a mistake.

"I have made a mistake," he said. "I need a manservant to buy bread at the baker's and vegetables in the market for me. Only then can I become completely invisible."

He made the rounds of the town to find a manservant who could buy bread for him and fetch the vegetables so that he could be completely invisible. He found many menservants, but none of them suited the old man. One was too young, another too lively, a third was garrulous and yet another was bent on sociability, companionship and amusement.

"I have made a mistake," said the old man again. "I must look for an old man, a quiet, solitary man, prepared to share my solitude. He must be a servant who is solely devoted to his master and pays no attention to anyone else."

The people told him that such a man existed. He lived in a secluded, abandoned house and avoided the company of his neighbors. It was said of him that he had come to the town recently and was looking for a master who would be prepared to share his solitude. The old man hastened to the house at once and as soon as the door was opened to him he saw that he had found his servant. A tall, thin man stood looking at him in silence.

"Friend," said the old man, "are you prepared to come into my service?"

"No," said the other, "I am looking for a master who, so I have been told, lives in a silent, lonely house not far from here. I have been looking for him for a long time, because I want to look after him."

"I am that master," said the old man joyfully, "come with me. You will find everything just as you have described."

The other smiled as if something in these words had entertained him.

"My hour has not yet come," he said. "I will be with you this evening. Have everything in readiness so that I can attend to you to the best of my ability."

The old man hastened home and made everything ready, so that he could be attended to as well as possible. Towards evening, the servant rang the bell.

"You are the last person I shall let in," said the old man, when he had shut the door behind him. "From now on, no one else will ever visit me."

Once again the servant smiled, as if something peculiar about these words had struck him.

"You are expressing my own desires," he said. "Seldom indeed have I found a master so much in keeping with my wishes."

"I must also tell you," said the old man, "that the fire has been put out and all the windows are shuttered. It may be hard for you, but all the time we live in this house, that is how it will be."

But the servant smiled for the third time.

"Never," he said in surprise, "have I met a master who understood my intentions so well. You will be satisfied with me, for I shall certainly attend to you this very evening."

And indeed, that very evening he was attended to.

The Meeting

IN a deep valley surrounded by high mountains lay a prosperous village. One day rain began to fall there. This was no ordinary rain. It was a solid wall of water which roared so mightily as it fell that both sight and hearing were cut off. The priest, looking out of the window of his old presbytery, thought: "Good for the grass," because he had a goat. But when it went on raining and the water rose to the creature's knees, he took his Bible and began to look through it until he had found the right place. Then he smiled, put the book aside and said: "The world is coming to an end," because that was what he had always said.

The rector stood looking out of the window of his new rectory. The water had risen to the window frame, and he too realized that something extraordinary was happening. He took his Bible and looked until he had found the place. Then he put in a slip of paper to mark the page and smiled. "The world is coming to an end," he said happily, because that had been the subject of his last sermon. He stepped into a boat which had been lying ready for this purpose for years and rowed over to see the Pope.

The Pope stood reading at the window of his bedroom, since the ground floor had already vanished under the water. He pushed up the window and pointed a finger at the text he had found.

"Here," he said with satisfaction, "here it is in black and white."

The rector stepped out of the boat into the room and looked over his shoulder.

"No, it isn't," he said. "What made you think of that? That refers to something quite different. Here, this is where you should be looking," and he showed him the page *he* had found.

The Pope took a step backwards and regarded him with astonishment.

"Do you mean that?" he asked. "Or are you making a joke?"

The rector, who seldom made jokes, felt offended, but he restrained himself, for the water was up to their ankles by now.

"We must ask the priest," he replied temperately. "Then you will hear the truth from someone else as well."

They rowed across to the priest, who by now had climbed onto the roof of his presbytery. But when they had explained the problem to him, he began to laugh heartily.

"Come now," he said, "you have *both* found the wrong page. Look, *here* it is." And he showed them where it was.

A deacon, who was just rowing past, heard this. He stepped onto the roof of the old presbytery, where the other three were already standing, and opened his Bible at once.

"Friends," he said, "we must reach agreement, for the water is almost up to our mouths. Look, it is *here,* where I have placed my finger."

And he showed them the page he had found while he was at home.

The other three looked at each other, shaking their heads. They had come across a good many things in their time, but never before had they met with such blindness. They would have explained this to the deacon, but the water was up to their mouths. And they were silent for evermore.

Now there was nothing between the high mountains except a still, unruffled lake. A dove flew over it. The bird circled above the water, as if looking for something. Then it flew away.

The
Proposal

ONCE upon a time there was a young frog who lived in a rubber ball, and he was terribly in love. But he did not dare to say so, because he was rather shy by nature.

Now, he knew an old frog who had already been married four times and therefore knew quite well how to say so. But he didn't altogether trust him. And so he swam up and down irresolutely until—how extraordinary—he just happened to brush up against him!

"What are you doing here, mister?" asked the old frog.

"Oh, just hanging around a bit."

"You are in love," said the old frog, looking him straight in the eye.

"Good heavens! How did you know that?"

The old frog smiled. "I have been up that road before," he said. "Sit down. Keep calm. It is perfectly normal. What's her name?"

"Not telling you."

The old frog opened his eyes wide.

"Why not?"

"Well," said the young frog, "because she is so beautiful. And if I told you, you might follow it up."

The old frog swallowed a bit of duckweed and looked the other way, because that was just what he had planned to do.

"Come," he said after a time, "just tell me. I am too old for such nonsense."

And the young frog told him her name and where she lived. "She's a treasure," he finished.

"Fine," said the old frog, "I'll arrange it for you, you'll see."

"How can I thank you?"

"A little gift," said the old frog, "anything you like. It needn't be much, as long as it's good quality." And he swam away.

Then the young frog caught a big bluebottle and took it back to the house of the old frog as a present. But when he passed the house of his treasure he was seized by a tremendous longing. He leaned the blue-bottle against a stalk and burst into tears. His treasure heard him, and looked out and saw her lover there. His bright stomach was gleaming in the moonlight and there was a greenish light in his bulging eyes. She came outside and asked, "What are you doing there, mister?"

He sighed and said: "I was taking a bluebottle to a friend who is going to help me in my desire."

Now it was her turn to open her eyes wide.

"He has just been here," she cried, "and he wants to marry me. But I said no."

"Good heavens!" cried the young frog. "And he came to ask on my behalf!"

So the words had been spoken at last, and they got married and went to live in the rubber ball. When the old frog passed by her house the next day he found it empty. He hurried off to his friend and rang the bell. The young frog opened the door himself and asked: "What are you doing here, mister?"

"My friend," said the old frog, "I have something awful to tell you. She's gone off with someone else."

"That's right," said the young frog, "and that someone is me."

The old frog opened his eyes wide. He swam silently to the surface and went to sit on a waterlily leaf. Just then a stork passed overhead. He asked nothing and he said nothing, but he snapped up the old frog and flew away, and the shadow of the bird fell over the rubber ball at the bottom of the ditch.

"Is something up?" asked the young frog. "You're blushing. Tell me about it."

"The stork has just passed," she said. "That's what it was."

And it was, too. Three weeks later, when their babies came into the world, their father told them this story and they told it to their children and at last it came to the point at which the story was printed and put on this paper. Here it is. Read it well. And when the great day comes, go to it yourself and don't leave it to anyone else.

The Innkeeper of Pidalgo

ONCE upon a time, in Pidalgo, in the County of Esquerra, there lived an innkeeper whom everyone regarded as eccentric. He considered it an honor to regale his guests with the best that was to be found in the district, giving them wonderful things to drink and refusing to allow even the most trifling deceit to be practiced in his bills.

All he charged for his wares was the profit necessary to keep himself and his wife alive, and he used the rest to purchase new pans, and skimmers of finer workmanship. If people ate an unusual amount he refused to accept any compensation at all, saying that the sight of such an eater was reward enough for him. At the great feasts he would stand in the doorway, rubbing his hands, his eyes aglow with delight and wandering pleasurably over his grateful guests. Once, at a dinner of dinners, he was seen to weep for joy.

It is not surprising that this inn was among the most popular in the County. Even from a distance you could recognize the little building from the food vapors rising above the treetops and the sound of knives on plates.

Cooks ran to and fro, their white caps standing out merrily against the green of the trees. Laughing faces were to be seen everywhere, with full mouths and bulging cheeks. Only rarely could you hear the tinkle of money. Generally the innkeeper nodded and waved his hands to indicate that this was an affair of a lower order, which could be settled the next morning.

Although all the food was prepared with the greatest of care, there was one dish which had carried the name of mine host into the farthest corners of the County. This was his roast. What he did with it no one knew. People forgot to think about it as soon as they had eaten a mouthful. It had a taste which was both mellow and spicy and there was no need to bite it: it melted by itself between tongue and palate. People would gladly travel by donkey to taste it and it often happened that strangers, spurning the art treasures of ancient Pidalgo, visited the town only to make the acquaintance of this outstanding dish.

Now it happened that through harvest failure and cattle sickness a great famine occurred in the County. The mills ceased to grind, the butchers hung their knives on the doorposts and the fires of the baking ovens went out. Only from the famous inn of Pidalgo did a plume of smoke continue to rise. As long as there was meat in the house, mine host presented his famous dishes. He could not refuse. If you asked him for a dish, he would get up and fetch it. He pulled the last vegetables from the kitchen garden, sliced open the belly of the one surviving pig and served up the great ribs of pork with a smile. But the scarity caught up with him too. After some time he had to put out the fires and turn off the tap. The inn was a sorry sight. The frying pans hung sparkling on the walls, and the shiny meat knife lay unused on the woodblock. No more smoke rose from the well-known chimney, no cheerful cries of cooks and maids resounded from the kitchens. A damp, sour smell hung in the unused dining room and gradually replaced the tempting cooking smells of the past. But the saddest sight of all was the innkeeper himself. Thin and pale, he wandered about the deserted house, lingering in all the spots associated with his greatest memories. He could stand staring for hours at a grease spot on the floor, or a shiny smear on the wall. It was neither hunger nor thirst which had made him thin. He would gladly have suffered far more, if only he had been able to entertain his guests in the old way. You see, that was the worst thing for him: to have to say no when a stranger passed by and looked inquiringly into the kitchen. To see the man go on his way, unfed and unrefreshed.

But even this did not last much longer. In the end people just passed by his inn, as they did all the others, without hope, without even looking up, as they would pass a house whose poverty was written on the window.

The famous host sat all day in the chair by the door, head sunk on his chest. In the evening he would close the shutters as usual and go slowly to bed. In the morning he would get up and sit outside his house again, like a condemned man, a criminal. Sometimes, as a step drew near, he raised his head, his eyes glinting with the faint hope that someone might stop and ask: "Do you still have those cutlets? Can you give me a leg of lamb?" But the people passed in silence.

Then one day a coach rolled up, drawn by six white horses. The coachman cracked his whip briskly, a red-cheeked footman jumped down from the back and opened the door. A well-nourished gentleman stepped out, with a distinguished smile on his fine, blooming face.

"Well," he said, "so you are the famous innkeeper of Pidalgo, in the County of Esquerra?"

"Yes, sir."

The unfortunate man had risen and was standing with difficulty, supporting himself on the back of his chair.

"Well then, tell me, what kind of strange country is this?" the gentleman continued, drawing his brows together in a frown. "They refuse to give me my favorite dishes. Only yesterday I ordered a cutlet and I was told that it was impossible, that there was famine here. What does this mean? Surely *you* have no truck with such foolishness?"

The famous innkeeper suddenly drew himself up to his full height.

"You are speaking to the innkeeper of Pidalgo, sir," he said.

The stranger nodded his satisfaction.

"Just as I told you," he said, turning to his companions, "this innkeeper has not his equal in the whole County. You have not disappointed me, mine host. Nor will I shame you: in seven days I will return to test your renown. You need not give me much. I am the foe of quantity and the friend of quality. Just produce a few excellent chops and some of your famous cutlets. You may expect ten guests. Goodbye!"

The coach rolled on. Next morning the innkeeper was no longer to be seen sitting outside. The shutters remained closed, the door was shut. People thought that the inn had been vacated, but on the seventh day a cloud of blue smoke spiraled from the chimney. Some hours later a wonderful smell of roasting filtered through the slats of the closed shutters. There was general astonishment in Pidalgo. People knocked at the door and tapped on the windows, but there was no answer.

Toward evening the coach rolled up. The duke and nine noblemen of his court descended, joking merrily, and walked once or twice around the closed house. They sniffed contentedly at the fine, savory smell which was making its way out through chinks and crevices.

"Come," said the duke, after waiting a little while to see if anyone was coming out to welcome them, "we had better go in."

He raised the latch of the door, pushed it open and stopped, pleasantly surprised, on the threshold. In the great dining room stood a table covered with a snow white cloth and adorned with lighted candles and fine glass. On the dishes lay the famous meat, roasted to a pale brown and excellent to look at. At the head of the table sat the innkeeper. He looked very pale.

"Gentlemen," he said in a weak voice, "since I have only just recovered from a severe illness, I do not feel capable of greeting you in a fitting manner, still less of serving you in the way which befits your rank and station. So don't take it amiss if a humble man sits among you in order to see that everything is according to your wishes. And although I cannot pass the dishes myself, I have chosen my seat in such a way that I shall be able to help you to the best of my ability."

The duke frowned for a moment; then he saw the reasonableness of these words. The roast smelled wonderful. The praise of his eating companions was unanimous and the duke himself did not stint his praises. He had visited many courts, he said, and he boasted a cook in no way inferior to any of theirs. But here he had found his master. Would he care to name the roast which had so far exceeded his expectations?

"Noble lord," said the innkeeper, after having stared in front of him in embarrassment for a few moments, "your words rejoice my heart and make me forget the sacrifices I have made in the preparation of this dish. But release me from the necessity of naming it and be so kind as to rest content with the assurance that I regard only the noblest food as worthy of your plate."

"Bravely spoken," said the duke, smiling. "Every cook has his secrets. Will one of you gentlemen be so good as to pick up my napkin ring, which has fallen under the table?"

One of the courtiers stooped and groped under the table. After a few moments he reappeared, his face chalk-white.

"What is it, Rodriguez?" asked the duke politely. "Have you seen a ghost?"

"No, my lord. A wooden leg."

That was the last meal prepared by the innkeeper of Pidalgo. He died soon afterwards and was buried at Las Casas, near Cordova.

Joshua

THERE was once a frog called Joshua. To be honest, Joshua was also a bit of a poet. Not a great one, but in his spare time he did write verses which were quite fit to be seen. He also sometimes composed little songs which he performed himself in a fine baritone while sitting on a water lily leaf. All these things were strange to the pond where Joshua lived. There were no other poets there. The others lived by catching gnats, ambushing a little beetle from time to time and leaping about in the sun. But never had anyone thought of making up verses. How had Joshua hit upon the idea? Who can say? God's ways are wonderful. But first of all, let us tell something about Joshua's appearance. In contrast to most poets, Joshua looked very agreeable. He had a white waistcoat with brown spots on it, and light green breeches which showed off his well-formed legs admirably, a green jacket and great, bulging eyes. It was actually his eyes which betrayed that he was a poet. There was expression in them. Somber is not the word. Melancholy comes a little closer. But if one were to describe the expression in Joshua's eyes in a word, that word would be—well, in German it would be "Weltschmerz"—but there just isn't one in our language. Homesickness, longing for another pool, or perhaps even for a higher life. Perhaps a longing not even understood: those are the most painful of all.

Later, when he was famous as far away as the duckpond, they said of him that he sometimes wept. Don't believe such gossip. How could you see someone crying under water? Others again felt he was cherishing a secret love. You see, people always want a definite reason for sorrow. But I tell you, a truly deep sorrow is as unreasoning as a truly deep joy. I tell you—no, I won't tell you any more. Joshua was pining away. He ate little at supper time; he generally sat staring silently over his plate.

116

"Joshua," his father said once, "you're leaving your food. What's wrong, my boy?"

"Nothing, father," said Joshua.

He left the table and swam upward with painful strokes. The moon shone silver on the calm water. It was a beautiful evening. Joshua sat down on a waterlily leaf and sang a song. It was a sorrowful song. I stood still, struck by it.

"Joshua!" I said. "How sorrowfully you sing! It makes me think that something pains you. And what do I see? You weep! Come, tell me! I too am a singer, I too am sorrowful. Likely I can understand you, even help you!"

I went on talking for a long time, in a calm, friendly voice. You see, I would have been able to give an answer to anything that Joshua had told me. But Joshua looked at me and shook his head. Then my heart also broke, and I cried. So we wept, the two of us. The moon floated across the water. It was a wonderful evening.

The King Who Did Not Want to Die

ONCE upon a time there was a king and he was going to die, but he did not want to. He hid his dead mother's watch under his nightshirt and thought to himself: "As long as it goes on ticking, nothing can happen to me." It chimed the hour, and the half-hour, and the king listened happily to the delicate tinkling. And again he thought: "As long as it chimes I shall live. For my mother did not want anything bad to happen to me."

The doctor heard him. He was a stern man. He came to the king's bedside and said:

"I have to say this. You are going to die."

The king was frightened. "I do not believe you," he said.

"No," said the doctor, "but it is true, all the same."

"When?" asked the king.

The doctor felt his pulse and put his ear to the sick man's chest. "It is still ticking," he said, "but faintly. When the leaves fall in the garden your time will come."

The king looked out of the window and smiled. The trees were still bare but for a faint green haze about their twigs, but spring had only just begun.

"You can go," he said, "and call my gardener here."

When the gardener came, the king was sitting up in bed and his eyes were sparkling.

"Gardener," he said, "I am not going to die."

"Sire," replied the gardener, "we must all die some time."

"Not I," said the king. "Cut down the trees which lose their leaves in autumn and replace them with fir trees, spruce and holly."

The gardener did as he was told. He cut and planted all summer, for it was a big garden. But when autumn came, everything was ready and not a leaf fluttered to the ground. The king was standing at the window in his nightshirt when he saw Death coming. Death looked round in surprise at the garden and shook his head. But he walked across it all the same and came into the king's room.

"I must fetch you tonight," he said, "yet not a leaf has fallen."

"Strange," said the king. "How can that be?"

"I know very well," said Death, "but it will not help you. Do you see that little weeping willow? It is quite brown. This evening a wind will come up and it will be bare. Why did you not cut it down?"

"I could not," said the king reluctantly. "It stands on my mother's grave."

Death nodded. "I knew that," he said. "It is a good thought, and for that reason I will tell you the exact hour. When the clocks strike half-past nine I will come to fetch you."

As soon as Death had gone the king summoned his ministers.

"Take the bells of the tower," he said, "and break all the clocks in the palace. Nothing must tick any more, and nothing must chime."

The ministers did as they were told and when evening came no one knew what the time was. The king was standing at the window when he saw Death drawing near. Death lingered a moment in the garden, as if listening for something, and shook his head. But then he crossed it and came into the king's room.

"It is time," he said kindly. "I have come to fetch you. But half-past nine has not yet struck."

"Strange," said the king, "how can that be?"

"I know quite well," said Death, "but it will not help you. Listen."

He held up his finger at the same moment the hidden watch tinkled under the king's nightshirt.

"Why did you not break *that* one?" asked Death.

"I could not," said the king awkwardly, "it was my mother's watch. She gave it to me when she died."

Death nodded. "I knew that," he said, "and it is a good thought. Did you love her so much?"

"More than anyone else," said the king, and his eyes filled with tears.

"Would you like to see her?" asked Death.

The king began to weep. "Do not torture me," he said. "It is my dearest wish."

Death nodded. "I knew that," he said, "and your wish shall be granted."

The door opened and the king clutched at his heart. His own mother was standing there. She leaned over him and whispered something in his ear.

"Mother," said the king, "I don't want to."

"You already have," she said. "And you willed it yourself."

The Naked Soul of King Pim

ONCE upon a time there lived a statue. Yes indeed, it was alive! No one knew it, except of course the statue itself. But it kept the matter dark. Never a blink from its stone eyes, never a thumb's breadth of movement in its lifted sword. And that, despite the fact that it had been standing for a hundred years!

Yes, King Pim had died a hundred years ago. He had been a bad king and he really shouldn't have had a statue raised to him at all. But he got one, and in the middle of the market place, too; and he himself lay in a bier in the cathedral, in an ermine cloak and embroidered slippers. It was a beautiful corpse, they said, and they were right. But his naked soul slipped out of his half-open mouth, rose upwards like an arrow and stood quaking before God's throne.

"It's naked," said the angels.

But the king straightened himself and said: "I am the king."

"So am I," said God, smiling.

"Yes," said the king, "but I am a real king."

"So am I," said God, smiling.

He raised his hand and at once there echoed the ravishing sound of a hundred thousand voices.

The king too raised his hand and cried: "Music!" There was complete silence.

"No," said God, "you mustn't do that. In any case, you are completely naked. Come back in a hundred years' time."

And in the same moment the king was standing on earth. He rubbed his eyes and looked around him in surprise. Yes, he knew this road, he had often traveled along it in his carriage. In the distance lay his residence, but some time had already passed and the snow was falling on his naked body. Fortunately, a tramp was strolling ahead of him.

"Here," said the king graciously, "you may give me your trousers. I am King Pim. And I need the jacket too. Look sharp now!"

But the man passed on in silence.

"Here, rascal!" cried the king, "don't you understand? Where are your manners. On your knees, at once!"

But the man turned the corner, humming a tune.

"Extraordinary," muttered the king, "deaf and dumb! I thought I had had them all hanged during my reign. Some administrative error, no doubt."

And he went on his way, shaking his head. But fortune favored the king again, for at the turn in the road he saw a second man walking ahead of him. He hastened his footsteps and soon caught up with him.

"Don't be frightened," said the king graciously, "I am the king. Don't worry, you can keep on walking. Yes, that's right. As you can see, I am naked. You realize that it won't do, the king naked and his subjects running about fully clothed. Take off your trousers behind that tree."

But this man too was silent. Then the king grew angry. He raised his fist and struck out. But how great was his astonishment when his hand fell through the man's shoulder! He stretched his length on the ground and a farm cart rattled over him. The king closed his eyes tightly, but he felt nothing.

"Well, that's nice," he said, laughing, "I am invisible and immaterial. I am nothing at all."

And he jumped up cheerfully and went on his way in high good humor; he took a special pleasure in not moving aside for people who came towards him but simply walking straight through them.

However, the closer he came to the capital, the greater became the crowds on the road.

"What can be going on?" muttered the king. He walked down the main street which was lined with policemen to right and left. Behind them the people stood waiting, at least eight deep. The king walked with his head up along the middle of the street, remembering former days; but in the end he began to feel uncomfortable, walking quite alone, and with a little effort of self-control, he joined the front row. In any case it was pleasant to think that he had a fine position, without getting in anyone's way. Because if you are nothing, you cannot get in anyone's way, that much is certain.

But what could be going on? The bells rang out glumly over the city and the flags hung at half mast from all the houses; if people had not been looking so excited one might have thought a minister had died. Suddenly there was a movement in the crowd; people pushed and shoved each other, but the king stood comfortably in the front row. He stretched

his neck and stared hard into the distance. Yes, there was something black coming. It seemed to be a funeral procession. Could it possibly . . . The king turned pale and quickly walked to the middle of the road. He could see clearly now: in front his own chancellor walked with measured step and solemn face; his twenty ministers followed, their heads high, but wearing black gloves; and behind them, yes, there was his own dear wife! She was crying, but in the whole procession—and it was a long one—she was the only one who was.

"Elizabeth!" cried the king. "Don't cry! I'm here."

But she passed by him in silence.

"Oh, God!" cried the king. "This is truly hard!" But no one heard him.

Then all his officials passed by, and all the courtiers and all the servants, and old Henry, his chamberlain.

"Here I am!" the king cried constantly. "I am King Pim!" But no one answered.

Then the king joined the end of the procession with the pallbearers and wept bitterly. For the length of three streets he walked behind his own corpse, and as he passed the people took their hats off and bowed low; but the king did not bow back because he knew they were bowing to the body and not to what was walking behind it.

And when the chancellor rode into the churchyard and made a speech which lasted two hours, and twenty gunners fired their cannon and all the people cried "Hurrah!" three times, the king was standing in the back row among the butchers' boys. Because he knew that all this was for the body and not for the soul which was standing among them.

Yes, that was a very uncomfortable day for the king. He wandered through the streets in his naked soul, sometimes stopping by the shops where people were selling furs. It was such a pretty sight to see. But in the main square he stopped in surprise: there was his own statue, large as life, with lifted sword!

"Well," said the king, smiling, "they've done that quickly! Smart work," and he walked around it thoughtfully. It really was a very fine statue, boldly upright, with the sword in one hand and one foot resting on three books. "Might and Wisdom" was inscribed on the pedestal and the king had to admit that both these virtues were very well represented. The only thing was that he could not remember ever having possessed them, but that did not affect the statue one way or the other.

The king sat down on the pedestal and thought. He had to spend a hundred years on earth. But—it was a strange thought—what if he were to creep inside the statue right away? It was hollow, and he had to stay somewhere, didn't he? After all, one is probably best off in one's own shell, that is where one is bound to feel most at ease. And what a fine position it was, in the heart of the city! Everyone passed by here—the processions were held here, the fireworks were let off here . . . .

"Yes, I'll do it!" cried the king suddenly.

And he did.

The processions were held and the fireworks were let off, and everyone passed by and the king saw it all and was happy to do so. The only thing he had to remember was that he was a statue and must not betray that there was a soul inside. That would have caused an uproar!

He watched the accession of the new king and his burial and he saw another four kings after that. All of them were very powerful and all of them died. In fact, this rather depressed the king and when he saw them riding past in their carriages he had great difficulty in not flourishing his sword and shouting: "Watch out! You are actually naked!" But he remembered that he was a statue and kept quiet.

So time passed, fifty years, sixty, seventy. After eighty years the king saw his own funeral procession for the second time, because the nation thought that it was not right for him to be in the churchyard; he would be better off in the cathedral. So he was buried in the cathedral; the king thought it was wonderful, because on Sundays the great doors opened and between the pillars he could just see his gravestone. It's always nice to know where you are.

So the years passed and the time left could be counted in months, then in weeks—and suddenly it was the last day, a Sunday. The king had died on a Sunday, he still remembered that well. His heart beat loudly behind his stone coat and if anyone had looked hard they would have seen the lifted sword trembling. But luckily no one looked, for after all he had been dead for a hundred years, and people soon stop looking.

The last hour was the slowest of all; the king kept his stone eyes fixed on the church clock; it was striking seven now and his soul had slipped out of his mouth at half-past seven, just a century before. The minute hand crept slowly on, slowly, so slowly, alas!

But while the king was counting the minutes, suddenly a great fear came upon him. Was he not still naked? Was he any better now than he had been a hundred years ago? Had anything changed at all? Yes, a grave in the cathedral and a statue in the square, but these things, as he now knew, were valueless when you stood naked and alone before the Light. And there were still five minutes to go!

Then a deep, deep despair overwhelmed the king; he could not think, he could not even count any more, he could only stare straight ahead at the cathedral. And through the great open doors he saw a little girl skipping in, with a red ribbon in her hair. She passed between the pillars, getting smaller and smaller, and stopped by the grave. The little girl hesitated for a moment, then clasped her hands before her eyes and prayed.

Just a short, simple prayer, and at the same moment the clock struck half-past seven and the king's soul rose straight up toward the Light.

The Princess with Freckles

ONCE upon a time there was a prince who was determined to get married, but he vowed that he would be wedded only to a very beautiful girl.

"All right," said the king, "there are plenty of girls about. I will summon *seven* every day, beginning tomorrow."

Next morning the first seven girls came to the palace. They really were very beautiful, for the king had selected them himself. He had enjoyed doing it.

"My dear boy," he said, "here they are. All golden-haired. Take your pick."

The prince put on the glasses which had been made specially for this purpose and looked curiously at the girls.

"No," he said, "not for me. The stuff looks like straw."

"All right," said the king, "tomorrow is another day."

Next morning another seven girls came in and they were even more beautiful than the first seven.

"Take it slowly, now," said the king, "you only get married once."

This time the prince took longer to consider, but not one of them really pleased him.

"All dark," he said. "They look like burnt toast."

"Never mind," said the king. "I'm glad you are taking it so seriously. If only I had done the same. We shall see what happens tomorrow."

The next day seven girls came into the palace with downcast eyes and blushing cheeks. They were embarrassed, not by the prince, but by their own beauty and did not know where to look.

"Bravo!" cried the king, "that's what I like to see! Now take your choice, my boy!"

126

The prince took seven hours over it, one for each girl. Then he looked at his father and shook his head.

"All red," he said. "They're just like fire."

This time the king frowned.

"Look here," he said sternly, "if I had dawdled so long, you would not be here at all. We will try once more, but tomorrow is the last day."

Now the seven most beautiful girls in the whole country were found. They were carried in in seven boxes and the king himself took off the lids and looked at them one by one. At the seventh box the king held his breath, for this girl had been chosen personally by his wife—and she was the one he liked best, too.

"This is the most beautiful," said the prince.

"I should think so!" said the king happily. "You see a girl like that only once in a lifetime. Take her now; you will never regret it."

"I don't know yet," replied the prince. "She will have to come out first."

The girl stood up and shook the woodshavings out of her rippling hair. The paper rustled as she stepped from the box and curtsied to the prince. Then she raised her arms above her head and turned around slowly so that she could be viewed from every side.

"Beautiful," said the prince, "really very beautiful. But what do I see?"

He stooped and peered at her right cheek through the special glasses.

"A little mark," he said. "What a pity."

Then the king was so angry that he boxed the prince's ears and ordered him out. He slammed the door of the palace and shouted through the key-hole: "Never come back again!"

The prince stood there in the pouring rain. Fortunately an old woman was passing by under a large umbrella.

"Well, Prince," she said, "what are you doing out here in the rain?"

The prince told her what had happened.

"Yes, yes," said the little woman, "these things happen; we can't all be perfect. What do you want to do now?"

"I want to shelter under your umbrella," replied the prince.

"All right," said the woman, "come underneath. And what else do you want?"

"I want to eat at your table and sleep in your bed. For I have nothing to live on and no roof over my head."

"All right," replied the old woman, "come with me. But you will have to do something in exchange."

"What must I do?" asked the prince.

The woman laughed to herself. "You ask too many questions," she replied. "You will just have to wait, and then you will see."

They walked together under the umbrella to the house of the old woman, who was really a witch. The prince did not have a nice time there at all. That night he lay on a straw mattress as hard as a board, and in the morning he had to make up the fire and eat burnt toast. The prince scarcely closed his eyes, for at home he slept in a swansdown bed. And next morning when he saw the burnt toast on his plate his face fell still more.

"Bah!" he said, "do I have to eat that?"

"Oh, no," said the witch, "you can leave it alone."

"Yes, but what will I have to eat then?" asked the prince.

The old woman laughed to herself again. "You ask too many questions," she replied. "Wait, and then you will see."

The prince waited for three days, but by that time he was so terribly hungry that he ate the black toast and enjoyed it very much.

"So black toast is all right now," said the woman. "And how are you sleeping?"

"I cannot get used to the straw," grumbled the prince, "it really is too much. Do I have to lie on it?"

"Oh, no," said the witch, "you can leave it alone."

"Yes, but where would I sleep then?" asked the prince.

The old woman laughed again. "You ask too many questions," she said. "Just wait, and then you will see."

And sure enough, after a week the prince was sleeping like a baby and liking it, too.

"So straw is all right," said the woman. "And how would you like to make up the fire now?"

The prince showed her his hands, which were covered with scratches and blisters.

"I will never learn that," he grumbled bitterly. "Must I *really* do it every morning?"

"Oh, no," said the witch, "you can leave it alone."

"Yes, but then how would I get warm?" asked the prince.

The little woman shook her head and laughed. "You ask too many questions," she said again. "You must just wait, and then you will see."

And sure enough, after a few days had passed, the prince could make up the fire without burning his hands, and he enjoyed it, too.

"So fire is all right," said the little woman. "And now that you have learned all that, you must do something for me."

"With pleasure," said the prince, who had grown rather more agreeable. "Must I do it at once, or shall I wait and see?"

"At once," replied the old woman. "I have a daughter, and she has freckles. She looks after the sheep and sleeps in a hollow tree. She is ashamed to show her face and that is why you have never seen her."

"Freckles are nothing to be ashamed of, surely?" said the prince.

"These things happen," replied the little woman, "we can't all be perfect. Now, I have prepared a magic ointment for my daughter and it is ready in a jar. But the jar is in the attic and I cannot fetch it. I have grown too old; my legs are not up to it."

"If that is all," said the prince, "I will do it for you gladly." And he climbed up to the attic and found the jar of freckle cream.

"Now you must look for her," said the little woman, "and when you have found her, rub the ointment on her face."

"Will the freckles disappear then?" asked the prince.

"I hope so," replied the little woman, "but I do not know for certain. For when I was making the ointment my mind wandered for a moment. These things happen and we can't all be perfect. Now, my boy, go!"

The prince went into the wood and looked behind all the trees. But he could not find the girl. When night fell he lay down on the moss and slept peacefully, for he had been sleeping on a straw mattress all this time and he was comfortable on the ground. The next day he crossed the heath. He looked behind every bush, but he could not find the girl. The prince grew hungry and ate currants and blackberries. He thought them wonderful, because all this time he had been eating burnt toast. And when evening fell he made a fire, for he knew how to do that now. All through the second night he slept contentedly.

Next day was the third day. The prince was just resting in the shadow of a big tree when he heard the tinkling of bells. He jumped up and saw a flock of sheep approaching. In the midst of them walked a girl. She turned pink when she saw the prince, for her face was covered with freckles, and she tried to run away through the trees, but the prince soon overtook her.

"Do not be afraid," he said. "I wish you well."

He smeared the ointment on her face and the freckles disappeared, all but one. It was only a tiny dot on her right cheek, but however hard the prince rubbed he could not get rid of it.

"It suits you," he said at last. "That one little mark shows how fair you are. Will you marry me?"

The girl was willing and so she said "yes" at once, for when you want something it is better to say so. Their wedding feast lasted for three days, and the princess wore such beautiful clothes that everyone was astonished, for she was only a poor little shepherdess. And stranger still, wood shavings fell from the pleats of her satin gown. Even stranger things were to happen. For the king had chosen as bridesmaids the same seven most beautiful girls that the prince had rejected. They came rustling out of their boxes, but when the seventh box was opened it was empty. Everyone was dismayed.

Only the old queen laughed to herself. "Such things happen," she said calmly. "And now we will go to the Town Hall." And she walked in the grand procession under her old umbrella, for we can't all be perfect. And when people asked why she was laughing, she replied:

"You ask too many questions. Just wait, and then you will see."

The Cloud Tree

ONCE upon a time there was a little boy who longed to be up in the clouds, because he had heard so much about them. He went to his father and asked:

"What does the world look like when you are up in the clouds?"

"Everything is white," his father answered. "And it is very, very quiet."

This pleased the boy. He climbed up into the attic and looked out of the window. But still he was not high enough. Far above his head the white clouds sailed across the blue sky and he could not reach them.

"I will plant a tree," thought the little boy, "and I will call it the cloud tree. And when it is big enough I will climb into its branches and reach the clouds from there."

He went out into the street where he lived, looking in all the gutters, and at last he found an acorn. He put the acorn in a flower pot and went every morning to see if the cloud tree was appearing. And one morning, there it was. It was hard to believe that a tree could grow from so tiny a plant, but the boy believed that it would. He put the pot on the window sill and before going to school he sprinkled a drop of water into the black earth. After three years the little tree was already so big that its roots cracked the pot. The boy planted the tree in the garden and forgot about it. For he himself was bigger now and he no longer believed in the tree. The clouds now seemed quite ordinary—and there was nothing above them. He had learned that at school and that was why he forgot the tree.

But the tree did not forget the boy. When it was still an acorn it had clearly heard a voice saying: "*You* will go up into the clouds," and it never forgot that voice. It thrust its roots deep down into the earth and stretched its little crown higher and higher towards the sky. "No one believes in me any more," it thought to itself. "But I will go on, because I was born to reach the sky."

The years passed and the tree grew bigger and bigger. The boy's father died, and his mother died, too. And the boy, who was now a grown man, stayed in the house alone. He walked through the garden and beside him walked a young woman. They were holding hands, for they wanted to get married, but they did not know it for certain yet.

"The tree must go," she said. "It keeps out too much light."

And the boy who was now a man stood still and looked at her.

"If that is what you want, so be it," he answered. "I planted it myself, but *you* are dearer to me."

Then she realized that he really did love her and threw her arms around his neck.

"The tree shall stay where it is," she said, "because it has brought light into my life."

Then he also knew that she truly loved him and they married and lived in the house.

"*I* did that," thought the tree to itself, and all its leaves rustled at the thought. But it did not forget the purpose for which it had been planted, and continued to grow vigorously.

One day the man who as a child had known the tree was walking through the garden with a little boy. He was now a father himself.

"What a tall tree!" said the little boy. "Where is it going to?"

"That is the cloud tree," replied his father, "for it is going up to the clouds."

And the little boy asked: "What does the world look like when you are up in the clouds?"

Then the father remembered what he had heard as a child and he answered: "Everything is white and it is very, very quiet."

This pleased the little boy. He had often wondered about the clouds and he longed to be up there. And every day before he went to school he gave the tree water from a little bucket which he kept specially for the purpose, and the tree thought this was wonderful and rustled its leaves. It grew and grew, but the little boy was growing, too, and he forgot the tree. The clouds became ordinary clouds and there was nothing above them. He had learned that at school.

But the tree did not forget the boy. Once the child had looked trustfully up at it, and it remembered that. It knew its destiny and thrust out its roots until they ran under the garden of the next house. Its truck grew thick and strong and its crown was as high as the house itself.

Now the boy was living alone in the house. His parents had died and he too had become a man. But he did not marry. He wanted to, but he could not find the right woman. For whenever he had found a girl he liked, she said: "That tree must go, it keeps out the light." Then he answered: "All right. I am fond of it, because my father planted it himself. But you are dearer to me." And then he would wait for the answer his mother had once given, for that would show that the girl truly loved him. But the answer never came. The girl would throw her arms round his neck and say: "I am glad that it is to be cut down, and that you are doing it for my sake." But he never did, for the tree was dearer to him, and so he did not marry.

One day he was wandering sadly through the garden, looking at the tree. The tree was sad, too. It had always brought good fortune, but now it was bringing sorrow. It rustled its leaves and whispered: "I would like to see another child that believes in me." But the man did not understand the rustle of the leaves. He took his knife and cut a heart in the bark of the tree, with an arrow piercing it. He took three days over the carving, for the heart was large and he cut deep.

And in the place where the heart was carved the tree sickened. In two years it lost all its leaves and in the third year it fell onto the house and the house collapsed. And in the ruins they found the man, but he was still alive.

When he opened his eyes he was lying in a white room. Everything was very, very quiet. A man in a white coat bent over him and felt his pulse, but said nothing. Then a woman came to his bedside and laid a hand on his forehead. She too was dressed in white and she too said nothing. "My father was right," thought the man. "I am in the clouds."

The woman did not leave his bedside. She brought him food and smiled at him. Sometimes he wanted to say something to thank her, but she put her finger to her lips and shook her head. "It doesn't matter,"

thought the man, "for I have found her now." And so he had, for when he was better he asked her if she would marry him and she said yes at once.

The house was rebuilt and a year later they had a child. "I'm still in the clouds," thought the man, "and my happiness would be complete, if only the old tree were still alive."

But it was still alive. For the baby's cradle was made of its wood and when he looked hard he could see on the panel over the child's head the heart that he himself had carved. He could see only the top half, and the arrow that had pierced the lower half was gone.

"Good old tree," said the man. "What great happiness you have brought me." His wife heard him and asked what he meant. But he never explained.

The Thrush Girl

ONCE upon a time there was a little girl who longed to be able to understand animals. She went to her old grandmother and said:

"Oh, grandmother, I would so love to understand the animals. Can you teach me how to do it?"

The grandmother could do a little magic, but not much.

"Oh, my child," she said, "I can only understand the thrushes, and that is not worth the trouble."

"It is enough for me," replied the little girl. "Please teach me."

So the grandmother taught the little girl to understand the thrushes. It was much easier than she had thought. She had only to be kind to the birds and throw them a few crumbs from time to time.

And when she had learned, she walked through the woods listening to the thrushes. Her grandmother was right. They had not much to say. But the little girl was right, too, because it was enough for her. And she went to her father and said:

"Father, bring in the hay, for it will rain tomorrow."

The father believed the child. He brought in the hay and by evening it was stacked in the barn. The next morning it began to rain. All the hay in the district was soaked and only his was dry. The father was glad he had listened to his child, but all the other farmers were angry. They were not pleased about the hay that had been saved; they thought only of their own loss. "That girl is no good," they said, "she will go to the bad."

But the little girl said nothing. She went back to her grandmother and said: "Now I would like to understand the moles as well."

"Oh, my child," replied the grandmother, "what a lot you want. Just be good to the animals, then you will understand them after a time."

135

It was three months before the little girl could understand the moles, too. And one day she said to her father:

"Bury the potatoes deep in the ground, for tomorrow it will freeze."

And sure enough, next day it froze. The father had buried his potatoes deep in the ground and they were undamaged. All the other farmers moaned and groaned, for they had not a single good potato left. He had warned them all, but they had not listened to him. They thought the little girl was bewitched. The little girl said nothing. Now she wanted to understand the language of the bees, too. Her grandmother could not help her, for she herself could not understand the bees.

"You know more than I now," she said. "You must learn to talk with bees in your own way."

So the little girl was very kind to the bees. She no longer ate honey, but left what there was in the hives. And after a little while she could understand exactly what the bees were saying to each other. And one day she went to her mother and said:

"Prop up the fruit trees in the orchard and lock the windows tight, for there will be a great storm tonight."

And that very evening a mighty wind rose up and devastated all the houses. The trees bowed and broke and there was great distress in the land. Only the orchard in which the little girl lived stood upright and not a tree was harmed. Other people grew so angry that they said:

"The child is bewitched! We will burn her!"

The people came running from every side with dry branches to build a great fire. The little girl stood on top of the pile of branches and called in a loud voice:

"Thrushes, thrushes, help me now!"

The people could not understand what she was saying, for it was in bird language, but the thrushes understood her perfectly. And in their thousands they flew down and each plucked a twig from the fire. The little girl was soon standing on the grass and there was no more firewood to be seen. She ran happily home and cried:

"Father, mother, the birds have set me free!"

Oh, how happy they were! But their joy did not last long, for the king's soldiers knocked at the door.

"Open!" they cried. "We have come to fetch the girl!"

She was taken to the market-place and there stood a man with a great gleaming axe.

"Your head must come off," he said. "Kneel down and stretch out your neck."

The little girl did as she was told, but as she laid her head on the block she cried in a loud voice:

"Bees, bees, help me now!"

The executioner did not understand her, for she spoke in bee language. But the bees understood her perfectly. And just as the executioner raised his axe, there came a loud humming and thousands of bees dived at him with their stings ready to strike. The executioner fell to the ground, dead, and the king's soldiers scattered in terror. The little girl ran home at top speed and cried:

"Father, mother, here I am! The bees have saved me!"

But now the king himself took a hand. He rang the bell and said: "I have come to fetch your daughter. I cannot kill her. But she shall be shut up in a stone tower."

So the girl was taken to a tower with walls fifteen feet thick. The windows had iron bars and the door was shut with three locks. It was so dark that she could see nothing, but she heard the rats and mice scuttling across the stone floor. The little girl sat on the ground and began to weep bitterly.

"I shall never get out," she said. "Oh, moles, moles, help me now!"

No sooner had she said this than thousands of moles began to tunnel under the tower. The walls began to tilt and topple. The floor burst open and the bars sprang out of the window-frames. And suddenly, crash! The tower fell with a roar that reverberated throughout the country. The king was just having breakfast when he heard it. He put down his knife and fork and said:

"The tower has fallen. Did you hear it?"

"Yes, father," said the prince. "Shall I marry her now?"

"I think you should," said the king, "although she is rather small."

And together they stepped into their coach with the four horses and rode at full speed to the house where the little girl lived. She was standing in the garden, scattering crumbs for the birds.

"Will you marry me, later on?" asked the prince.

"No," said the little girl, "I will not. I do not like the people here. I shall go away."

She packed three jam sandwiches in her basket and added a few blackcurrants. Then she put on her fur-trimmed cloak and went away. And no one ever saw her again.

The Secret

ONCE upon a time there were three gnomes who lived together in a hollow under an old chestnut tree. It was very comfortable. There was a sofa, a tick-tock clock, a hearth to cook things on, a table and three little chairs to sit on.

In the next room there were three beds, as big as cigar boxes, and three chests as big as matchboxes. They had a little garden, too; there they grew dandelions and daisies and also a cactus, which prickled. The gravel on the path was as white as snow and much smaller than ordinary gravel. The dandelions and daisies were much smaller than they are in the rest of the world, too. And in the chicken run there were very tiny chickens which laid eggs the size of beads. They had bantams too, but the eggs *they* laid could not be seen by human beings. Only a gnome could say: here's another bantam egg!

The youngest gnome, whose name was Bill, did everything in the garden. He raked the gravel, picked the flowers and grew the grain for the chickens. He also collected the eggs in a basket and whenever a chestnut fell on the roof, he mended the hole and sawed the chestnut into pieces. He was the most energetic of the three.

The second was called Will. He swept the house and baked pancakes on the hearth. Sometimes, when it was someone's birthday, he made a suet pudding. He couldn't cook anything else; but the gnomes were quite happy with that.

The third gnome did nothing. He was the eldest and he smoked cigars on the sofa. Sometimes he read aloud from a book. The book was called *Hints for Lovers* and Bill had found it in the wood one day in October. He had immediately realized that there would be things of importance in it and every evening they listened to the eldest gnome reading pages from it. In the end they knew it by heart and yet they were unable to understand what a lover was. Will thought it was something to cook and Bill thought it was something to put in the ground.

But the oldest gnome said it was too difficult to understand. You shouldn't try to understand everything, he said. So they lived on, in happiness and contentment.

One evening when they were reading the book again, there was a tap at the window.

"Yes?" called the eldest gnome.

"I'm lost," called a voice as sweet as a bell.

The eldest gnome placed his beard between the pages to mark the place and said:

"It's Bill's turn to go outside." And Bill lighted his little lantern and went out.

"I'll be right back," he said.

But he did not come back. Soon it was nine o'clock, then ten o'clock, and when yet another hour had passed the clock struck eleven. The other two gnomes became very worried.

"I do hope an acorn hasn't fallen on his head," said one.

"Perhaps he has walked into a twig," said the other. Then they waited in silence.

At last Bill came back. His eyes were shining, but he said nothing. Now everything was different. The chickens got dirty, the dandelions grew up to the window and the cactus grew so large that it was dark inside the room.

"He's ill," said the eldest gnome to Will. "You go and collect the eggs. I will rake the gravel and pick the flowers. It will soon pass."

But it did not pass. Bill stayed away more and more often and in the end he did not come back at all. They left his chair where it was and put his plate on the table every day, but he had gone, and he stayed away. The eldest gnome read from the book in the evenings, although they knew it by heart. But things were not as they had been and the old gnome fell ill. A week before Christmas he died. Will buried him in the garden and stayed in the house alone. He baked, swept, raked and read from the book which he knew by heart. But things were not as they had been and he too fell ill and died.

Then the house was empty. The book lay open on the table and the spiders spun their webs over the three plates. The three beds stood in the little room at the side and the clock ticked and struck the hours, weeks and months. And when many months had passed, Bill, the youngest gnome, came back. He went around the house calling and clapping his hands, but there was no one to answer him. Then he came to live in the house with his wife and child. They ate from the three plates and slept in the three beds and in the evening the gnome told them how things had been before. But he did not read the book again; after all, he knew it by *heart*.

The Death
of the
Storyteller

ONCE upon a time there was a storyteller who was dying. All his life he had told stories about gnomes and now, before he died, he wanted to see a gnome, a real gnome. He looked in the store cupboard, in the biscuit tin and under the sideboard, but there wasn't a gnome to be seen. The storyteller began to cry:

"Oh, dear God," he said, "they're finished. There is not a single one left! All my life I have firmly believed that there were gnomes, but now what am I to think? That greengrocer next door who always laughed at me was right, after all. Now there is nothing more to hope from life."

And the storyteller crept into bed, blew out the candle and waited for death.

But Death did not come; he had taken the wrong turn and was only now grumbling his way around the house.

"Does the storyteller live here?" he called through the window.

"Yes, Death!" said the storyteller from his bed, "come right in! Be quick about it! All pleasure is at an end for me. Look out for the doorstep, there's a plank loose just inside."

"You're a strange one," said Death, bending over the bed, "were you waiting for me? People are always afraid when I come in. Are you glad that I am here?"

"Oh yes," said the storyteller, smiling, "I'm very glad, Death. The gnome won't come, that's why I'm pleased to see you. It's either the one or the other."

"What's all this about a gnome?" asked Death in surprise. "You're a real storyteller, you are. Better examine your conscience, remember your sins and think of eternity. Those are useful thoughts. I'll hang around in the garden for a while and you can tell me when you have finished."

The storyteller lay on his back gazing at the ceiling and did his very best to think about his sins and eternal punishment. But it didn't go well; there was always the thought of the gnome getting in the way.

"Dear Lord," he prayed at last, "I am but a poor storyteller with little understanding. Do not be angry at my wish, the only one I have: please let me see a gnome."

But no gnome came. The storyteller waited and waited; then he turned his head and looked through the window; Death was standing there beside the rose bush, nodding at him.

"Come in," called the storyteller, "come in, Death!" And Death came and took him in his arms and laid him at God's feet.

"Who is this?" asked God.

"This is a storyteller," Death replied, "he has just died."

"What was his last thought?" asked God.

"He wanted to see a gnome," Death replied awkwardly.

God smiled.

"That was a very good thought," he said. "For that, you may let him in."

The Small Kingdom

THERE was once a very foolish king. All the kings round about were nastier than he, and as each in turn seized a portion of his kingdom, it grew smaller and smaller, until all he had left was a piece of land no bigger than a public park, and that he had to keep, otherwise he could no longer have remained a king.

The king had three sons even more foolish than himself. The eldest had the most sense. He could not count up to ten, but he could count up to three. The middle one, by going to evening classes, had got as far as two, and the youngest could not count at all. Now, none of this would have mattered if the king had possessed a large kingdom, but because it was so small he worried. And when he felt that his end was approaching, he called his three sons to him.

"My sons," he said, "it is well known that I am a foolish king."

"Yes, father," answered the three sons. For they were not too stupid to be aware of that.

"It is also well known," resumed the king, "that you are more foolish by far."

The three princes nodded. For this truth had come to their ears.

"Well, now," said the king, "my kingdom is not large. I can easily see it all from my window. But, with good sense, something can still be made of it."

"To be sure, father," answered the princes, "but good sense is just what we have not."

The king sighed. "All right," he said, "then divide my kingdom among yourselves and try to live on air."

So saying, he closed his eyes and died.

The three sons buried their father in a corner of the kindgdom and sat down at a round table.

"He said three things," said the eldest, who could count up to

143

three."And the first was, that with good sense something could be made of the kingdom."

"But that is just what we have not," said the middle one, who could count up to two. "But then he said two more things. And one of them was that we must divide it among ourselves."

"That is no good," said the youngest, "for we can only add up, not divide. But he also said that we must live on air. So let us do that."

And he stood up, said farewell to his two brothers and went away. The two that were left looked at each other and smiled.

"The air is quite still," they said. "He will not succeed."

But the youngest prince crossed the frontier cheerfully and there he met a miller who was looking for a man to help him.

"Hallo!" cried the miller. "What do you do for a living?"

"I live on air," answered the prince.

"So do I," said the miller. "Would you like to come and work for me?"

So the youngest prince went to work for the miller. He worked hard, for he was not lazy. And when a year had passed the miller was struck down by one of the sails of his mill. He lay still in the place where he had fallen and said to his helper: "My life is over. I have not much, but what I have is yours. I bequeath you the wise old bird that lives in the top of the mill. Be careful with it, for the bird has something that you have not."

And so saying, the miller closed his eyes and died.

The prince buried him at the foot of the windmill. Then he tied a black band round his head as a sign of mourning, put the bird on his shoulder and set out into the wide world.

Now, as luck would have it, the Emperor of China was making a journey on that very day. His mood was sorrowful, for he had no children and he wanted some very much. He had taken a jester into his service to cheer him up, but the fool was not one of the best. He tinkled his bells and stood on his head very well, but he was not really funny. He only told jokes that he had read in a book, and as the emperor already knew the book from cover to cover he was bored. So when he saw a man coming with a band round his head and a bird on his shoulder, he order the coachman to stop.

"Hey, there!" he called. "Who are you?"

"I am a prince," said the prince, and so he was.

The emperor smiled. "A pretty thought," he said. "And what do you live on?"

"On air," answered the prince, and so he did.

The emperor laughed heartily. "Extraordinary," he said good-naturedly, "really extremely good. And where is your master?"

"Gone with the wind," said the prince truthfully.

"Remarkable!" said the emperor. "But why is your mourning band not on your arm?"

"Now that he's gone, I have to use my head," said the prince, and that was true, too.

"This fellow is much better than my own fool," said the emperor, "and he's not using a book, either. I wish I had more like him."

"He has two brothers," said the bird, who was well aware that the prince could not count up to two, "and they are even better."

The emperor was delighted. He told the prince to get into the coach, and they drove straight for the kingdom of the three brothers. It had grown even smaller than before, for the kings round about had seized some more of the land, leaving a piece as big as a flower garden. Here in the middle the two brothers still sat at the same round table, pondering.

"What are you doing there?" asked the emperor curiously.

"We have been busy dividing the kingdom for a whole year," they replied. "But it is always growing smaller and then we have to start all over again."

"Jump into my carriage!" cried the emperor. "You really are even better than your brother!"

So it was that the three brothers came to live in the emperor's palace. They gave the most foolish answers to all questions, but everyone thought they were doing it on purpose, so they were a great success. And they really were living on air, just as their father had told them to do.

But the old jester grew very sad. He tried so hard to be amusing that he was no longer funny at all. He bought some new books and learned the most complicated jokes by heart and in the end he became so clever that no one could understand him. He took to wandering sadly through the palace in his jester's cap, shaking his head until the bells tinkled. The three brothers, though they were stupid, were also very kind, and felt sorry for him.

"Can we do anything for you?" they asked.

"Oh," said the old jester, "no one finds me funny any more; I have become too learned. I would like a little garden of my own in which to spend my last days, but that cannot be, for all the land belongs to the emperor."

"*We* have a kingdom. Come with us," said the princes. "But we must hurry, for it is getting smaller all the time."

And when they reached their kingdom, it had become as small as a bedspread. They walked up the garden path with the jester and his eyes widened with wonder.

"Is it mine?" he asked. "May I walk in it?"

That he could, for it belonged to him. He walked right across his own little garden and his bells tinkled because he was happy with himself, and that is the real happiness.

"This is just what I wanted," he said. "I thank you from the bottom of my heart."

And he went off at a smart pace to the emperor, laid his fool's costume before the throne and danced out of the palace.

"We are rid of him," said the emperor with relief. "How did you manage that?"

"We led him up the garden path," answered the eldest prince, "and then he walked into it with his eyes wide open."

"Anyone who can make a fool of a fool has plenty of sense," said the emperor. "Listen, I will make you my sons. But you must promise me one thing: swear that you will not become too learned."

The princes promised, and they kept their word. And the emperor was delighted, for now he had three sons who were extremely learned and did not show it. Each received one third of the Kingdom of China and that is a very large portion indeed. And the bird, who was well aware how foolish they were, held its peace and said nothing. That is unusual in this world and so he really proved himself to be a wise old bird.

Donkeys
and
Camels

ONCE upon a time there were two brothers who thought: "If we two go out into the world together, nothing can stand in our way."

And what they thought, they did, for they were not idle. Their old father went a little way with them, and then he said:

"Boys, I will go no farther. And now I will give you some more good advice."

The two brothers sat down on the grass at once, for their father always spoke for a long time. This time he spoke for two hours and when he had finished the eldest said:

"Many thanks, father, but now it is really time for us to go, for we want to do many things."

Their father answered: "I am very glad that you have listened for so long. Was the advice good?"

"No, father," said the younger, "and we shall not be following it."

"Quite right!" said their father, greatly relieved. "And now, my boys, forward!"

The two brothers stepped out manfully and soon they came to an enchanted castle. They knocked at the door and it was opened by a camel.

"May I guess?" said the elder brother. "You have not always been a camel?"

"Quite right," replied the creature sadly, "I have been under a spell for years. Will you follow me?"

He went ahead of the two brothers to a great hall where two donkeys were standing.

"The king and queen," said the camel. "I need say no more."

The king nodded. "Our situation is very, very disagreeable," he said, "and it has been going on for such a long time."

"How did it happen?" asked the elder brother.

The king plodded to and fro. "I will tell you," he said at last, "for there is no point in being silent. We have not always been donkeys. We are bewitched."

"But all the same," said the camel, "we have the courage not to give up."

"Of course," answered the king. "We have to solve a riddle: 'It is white. And when you drop it, it is yellow.' "

The elder brother smiled. "An egg," he said.

At that instant the castle shook and the king stood before them in his own shape. He was a dignified man in an ermine cloak, and the queen looked stately, too, although she was wearing glasses.

"Fancy my not being able to think of that," said the monarch, shaking his head. "We really *were* donkeys. You will stay to dinner?"

The brothers were very glad to, for they were hungry. They ate what was put before them and it was excellently cooked. No wonder, for the camel had turned back into a chef. Only two little bumps on his back bore witness to his past.

After the meal the king said:

"You two should go far. And now, listen! My stepmother, the old Princess Iodora, is living on a hillock of glass and cannot get down. At the same time, nobody else can get up. If you can find a solution to that, she will reward you richly."

The two brothers got up next morning before dawn, for the glass boulder was far away, and heavy indeed was the chest of gold pieces which the king had given them as a farewell gift.

Late that evening, when the sun was already dipping towards the horizon, they saw the rock. The rays of the setting sun were reflected in the glassy surface, which Princess Iodora's subjects were vainly trying to climb. Each time they slithered down again, and the princess herself stood weeping on the top, wringing her wrinkled hands. The two brothers watched silently for some time and felt very sorry for her. Then the elder turned to a window-cleaner, who was in charge of the work, and asked:

"Friend, have you a ladder?"

The man looked at him in surprise. "I am a window-cleaner," he replied. "Of course I have a ladder. What do you want with it?"

The elder brother smiled. "That is my secret," he said. "Just bring the ladder here."

The ladder was brought and the two brothers climbed up it. They picked the princess up and carried her to the ground. The servants stood speechless.

"You two should go far," said the princess, "for I have been standing here for five years and no one has ever thought of that before. What did my stepson give you?"

"A chest full of gold pieces," said the brothers.

"Not enough," said the princess. "I will give you three. Will you stay the night?"

The brothers were glad to, for they were very tired. They slept in feather beds and the next morning the princess herself took them to the palace gates.

"Many thanks," she said, "for without you I would be sitting up there still. And perhaps you would like to help my sister, who is also in great difficulties."

The brothers, who were extremely kind men, promised to do so, although this sister lived on the far borders of the kingdom. Her name was Princess Edelweiss, and she came to meet the two men from a long way off. The brothers were exhausted, for they had been carrying the four chests of gold all day and could scarcely stand up.

"You must help us!" cried the princess desperately. "We do not know what to do!"

The brothers sighed. "Tell us about it, then," said the younger, for by now it was he who had the most strength left. "But do it quickly, for we can do no more."

The brothers were taken to a hall in the palace, where a great crowd had gathered. These people were busy trying to open a locked door, but without success. The door of wrought iron, reinforced with copper bands, resisted the strongest locksmith.

"Behind that door," said the princess, sobbing, "is my daughter. That is the provision store and she wanted something tasty—I forget what. The door slammed to behind her, and that was two weeks ago."

The two brothers watched the strongest of the serving men trying to ram the door in with an oak beam, and they were seized with profound pity. At last the elder turned to the treasurer and asked:

"Have you the key to this door?"

The man smiled, for he thought this question very silly indeed.

"I keep all the treasures of this house," he answered, "so of course I have the key. What do you want with it?"

The elder brother shook his head. "That is my secret," he said. "Just bring the key here."

The key was brought. It fitted the lock exactly and the next moment the girl rushed weeping into her mother's arms. The people fell back in dismay, for it had never occurred to them to use the key, and even the princess was astonished.

"You two should go far," she said. "What did my sister give you?"

"Three chests full of gold," the brothers replied weakly.

"Not enough," said the princess, "I will give you six. But first of all you must both go and have a good sleep."

The brothers were delighted to hear this, and they slept like babies. When they awoke next morning Princess Edelweiss was sitting on the edge of their bed.

"Perhaps it is too much to ask," she said, "and you can say no if you like, but my Uncle Ferdinand is at the end of his tether."

The brothers felt refreshed after their sleep and answered:

"Come, Princess Edelweiss, tell us all about it."

The princess heaved a sigh and said:

"By mischance, he turned a tap and now the whole palace is under water. Can anything be done about it?"

The brothers thought for a moment and answered: "We suspect it can."

The princess embraced the brothers and accompanied them personally to the edge of the town.

"There is still a long way to go," she warned, "for my uncle lives across the desert, and that is three days' journey. Are you sure you do not need anything?"

"Nothing, good lady," answered the brothers. "We will find the way all right."

So they began their journey. They had ten chests of gold to carry and each carried five. Half way through the second day the elder brother sank down on the sand and said: "I can go no farther." And he closed his eyes and died. The younger thought to himself: "Now I have ten chests to carry. But where there's a will there's a way."

He loaded the ten chests onto his shoulders and took a few steps forward. Then he also fell forward into the sand and died.

A camel driver found them both the next day.

"What donkeys they were!" thought the man. "I would have loaded all this on my camels for one piece of gold. And yet the idea never occurred to them."

He shook his head, loaded the gold on his camels and went his way.

A Pair
of Wings

ONCE upon a time there was a man who longed to fly, not in a balloon, and not in an airplane, but with wings of his own. He had a special purpose in mind, but this he would tell no one. So he bought a dead swan and cut off the wings. He tied the wings on his arms and jumped out of a window. He had plenty of time to think it over in the hospital.

"Doctor," he asked at last, "are there any birds larger than swans?"

The doctor, who had done a lot of thinking himself, replied: "No. But there were once. I know of a museum where there is one."

As soon as he was better the man went to the museum. There was no one there, for it was simply a storehouse for extinct animals. In the last hall he found the bird. It was mounted on a stand and its head reached the ceiling. "I must have that one," thought the man. He cut off its wings and tied them to his back. Then he pushed the window open and stepped out. He had plenty of time to think it over in prison.

"Jailer," he asked, "are there any birds bigger than the ones that don't exist any more?"

The jailer, who had not thought at all, went at once to the governor. They talked it over together and when the man had completed his sentence he was sent to the madhouse. This place was run by kindly monks. They left the madmen in peace and gave them everything they wanted. Only, if they wanted something *too* crazy, the monks would say: "Tomorrow, perhaps," for tomorrow is another day. So they gave the man twelve feather mattresses, twelve eiderdown cushions and some cloth. He spread out his materials in the courtyard and began to sew two wings. They reached from the barred gate at the entrance, half way to the stone pump in the middle of the yard. He spent the whole summer on his preparations, but when autumn came everything was ready.

Now in the house there lived an old monk whose window looked

152

out on the courtyard. He had cared for the madmen all his life and had come to believe that people were just the same on the other side of the wall as on this side. When the old monk reached this conclusion, the governor of the madhouse said he must begin to take things more quietly. So he spent the whole day watching as the two wings grew larger and larger. Although he was a holy man, he could not restrain his curiosity. He opened the window and asked:

"Have you finished now?"

The man below took a step back and looked at his work. The two wings shimmered in the sunshine, for it was a mild day.

"Yes," he said, "they are finished."

He tied the wings to his back and began to flap them. But he did not rise. He remained on the earth as before. Tears sprang into his eyes as he looked at the monk.

"I cannot make them any larger," he said.

"You could become a little lighter yourself," the monk replied.

The man's face began to shine as if the thing were already done.

"How can I do that?" he asked.

"Eat little," answered the monk. "I have been doing it for years."

The man began to eat very little and grew thinner and thinner. Now and again he would tie the wings on and leap across the courtyard, but he never rose into the air. Yet he jumped higher and higher, for he had grown so light.

"You are coming on," said the old monk. "I myself have not got further than that. Can you not move your arms more vigorously?"

"No," said the man, "I am too weak now."

And so he was. He had grown so light that an old man could have picked him up, and the old monk did so. He put him to bed, saying:

"You are as light as a feather now."

"I can do no more," said the man. "I spent two years in a hospital and then another five years in prison, all for nothing. And how long have I been here?"

"Just three years," replied the monk, "and I have lived here all my life. But still, you have got further than I have."

"It has cost me a great deal," said the man, "but I have not succeeded."

The old priest took the sick man's hand and looked out of the window. It was late autumn, but the sun still shone in the courtyard. The wind blew the dry leaves across the cobbles and because it had rained overnight the threads of the wings had come undone. The feathers were blowing about.

"Are they all right?" asked the sick man, without raising his head.

"Oh, yes," said the old man, "rest easy. But what was it you really wanted to do?"

The sick man was tongue-tied. For it happens sometimes that a man may give up his whole life to something and yet come to doubt its value in the end.

"I have never told anyone," he replied. "I wanted to go to heaven without dying."

The other nodded, for that was just what he had thought.

"Everyone wants to do that," he said, "and in days gone by it used to happen. You are not mad at all."

The sick man smiled, for that was just what he had always known.

"I am glad to hear it," he said. "Don't let go of my hand, for I am going to sleep."

He closed his eyes and slept. The window was open and the feathers fluttered through the room. They fell on his thin body and lay softly on his closed eyes. But he did not notice. He slept.

The King in His Undershirt

ONCE upon a time a king was running through a cornfield. He did not do it from love of the country or because he wanted to know if his subjects' corn was growing well. He did it entirely for pleasure. It was delightful to see all the ears which came up only to his hips and which bowed to the ground as he flew over them like a breeze.

"How mighty a king is," he said with a smile. "Not only people but ears of corn bow before me! Everyone knows his place."

Now it happened that half way through his walk he felt the need

which we all feel at times. The king looked around for a hiding place, but there was none. Then his eye fell on the corn.

"Fair enough," he said, "I'll go in there. I may crush a few ears, but I am the king." So he hung his ermine cloak on a willow, took off his crown and stepped into the corn.

A few moments later a farmer passed by.

"Hey there, you vandal!" cried the farmer. "What are you doing, squatting there?"

The king turned red with anger, but as he had not finished he looked sternly at the other, sitting on his hunkers.

"Lost your tongue, varmint?" shouted the farmer furiously. "Isn't it enough to go treading my corn down, without making it filthy as well?"

"That is not the way to address your prince," replied the king with dignity.

"You're a filthy fellow!" shouted the farmer, coming right through the corn towards him. "A filthy fellow in an undershirt! A trespasser with no trousers on! Get out of here!"

And he called up the other farmers and together they chased the king through the cornfield with their clubs.

At the entrance to the village, however, a soldier cried: "It's the king! Attention!" And presented arms.

The farmers were ashamed and awaited their fate with bowed heads. But the king was more ashamed still. He crept back to his palace, pondering the fact that without his ermine he was just a man in an undershirt.

The Stolen Heart

ONCE upon a time there was a very poor fisherman. He had a wife and six children and a seventh was on the way. They lived together in a little house on the shore of a lake, and every morning the fisherman cast his nets, but since he caught little, his family was usually hungry. And because he loved his wife and children very much this made him sad.

One evening the fisherman hauled in his nets and looked gloomily at his catch.

"That is not good," he said. "If only I could catch more."

"You could," said a voice behind him.

The fisherman turned and saw a fine gentleman. He was sitting in a coach and blowing on his hands as if he felt cold. The fisherman shivered, for he too was suddenly very cold.

"Who are you?" he asked.

The gentleman smiled. But his eyes did not smile and he continued to look sharply at the fisherman.

"I will not tell you," he said. "Sell me your soul and you shall wallow in riches."

"How can I sell my soul?" asked the fisherman.

"You have only to breathe into my mouth. Then it will be done."

"And what shall I get for it?"

"Everything."

The fisherman thought. And as he thought, it was as if a cold wind blew about him.

"You are the Devil!" he exclaimed.

The man in the coach bit his lip. The smile died on his face and his eyes flashed.

"Sell me your soul," he said, "and you shall wallow in riches."

"All right," said the fisherman.

The gentleman stepped down from the coach and stood before the fisherman.

"Open your mouth," he said, "and blow your breath into mine."

The fisherman blew his breath into the stranger's mouth and at the same moment he felt a chill where his heart belonged.

"What have you done to my heart?" he asked fearfully.

The stranger smiled. His wan cheeks were suddenly tinged with pink and he looked at his frozen fingertips.

"They are tingling already," he said, "and I can feel life coming into my feet as well. In ten years you can recall me. If you want me, I will come, but you will not want me. You will have your reward."

He jumped into the coach and whipped up the horses. The fisherman watched him until he was out of sight and then rolled up his net to go home. But in the meshes of the net he saw an oyster. He opened the shell and inside it he found a great, gleaming pearl. He put it in his trouser pocket and went home. The children were sitting at the table and his wife was leaning over the cradle, for the new baby had just been born. She threw her arms round his neck and kissed him. Then she stepped back.

"How cold you are!" she cried in amazement.

The fisherman unloosed her arms and pushed her away from him.

"Call the mayor," he said shortly. "I have found a pearl."

The mayor came. And when he saw the pearl lying on the table he had difficulty in hiding his excitement, for it was the largest pearl he had ever seen.

"Not bad," he said casually, "but still only middling. I will give you a piece of land for it."

The fisherman exchanged the pearl for a piece of land that was no larger than the garden behind his own little house. But next day, when he put his spade into the ground, he struck the lid of an iron chest. And one again he went to the mayor and said:

"I have found treasure."

This time the mayor did not dare to say that it was not much, for the chest was full of diamonds and precious jewels and only the king was rich enough to buy the treasure. In return for the jewels, the king gave the fisherman three ships, each with a hundred sailors on board.

The ships sailed off with a great fleet of other merchant ships, but in the middle of the ocean a mighty storm blew up, so that half the fleet sank beneath the waves. But the three ships were among those spared. The remainder were taken by pirates. They plundered the holds, drove the sailors overboard and set fire to the rest. Only the three ships which belonged to the fisherman escaped, and returned to land filled with grain.

There was a famine in the land, because nearly the whole fleet had been lost. The fisherman sold his grain for ten times its price and now he really was wallowing in riches, but he did nothing for his family. He bought the king's palace, leaving the king a single room for himself. The fisherman sat on the balcony in a straw hat and smoked cigars in the sunshine, for he no longer had anything to do. In the street below the balcony people stood and begged for bread. But the fisherman laughed at them.

"If you can pay for it!" he shouted down to them. "Not otherwise!"

This was too much for the king. After all, he was still king. He came to the fisherman in his dressing-gown and said:

"Listen, this cannot go on. All the people are dying, and soon I shall have no more subjects."

The men down in the street held their breath. What the king had said was true and they had never thought of it before.

"What is that to me?" answered the fisherman. "I am comfortable here and I want for nothing."

Then the king grew angry. He had never been angry in his life before, but now he was.

"Do you know what is wrong with you?" he cried. "You have no heart!"

The fisherman turned pale. "How did you know that?" he whispered.

"A child could see it," said the king. "The people are falling down dead in the street and here you sit on your balcony, smoking cigars. I call that heartless. For what am I to live on if no one pays taxes? It looks to me as if you have sold your soul to the Devil."

The fisherman turned as white as a sheet. "How did you know that?" he asked again.

Now the king was frightened. "What!" he cried. "You didn't *really* do that, did you?"

The fisherman stared silently at the marble floor. "Yes," he said at last. "And that is why I sit in the sun all day. I am cold. Feel."

He took the king's hand and laid it on his chest. The king snatched his hand away quickly, as if he had touched a piece of ice.

"Go away," he said. "I do not want to see you here any more."

And he went to the edge of the balcony and leaned over the railing.

"My people," he said, "this man has sold his soul to the Devil. He is leaving my palace now and coming down. Let him go unhindered. No one is to touch him. And the grain will be distributed among you."

The fisherman came out through the door into the street and the people gave way before him. Not a word was spoken, not a hand lifted against him. As he walked through the town, everywhere the shutters were pulled tight and the doors locked. When he tried to greet someone, the other would drop his eyes and pass quickly by. The news that he had sold his soul to the Devil flew from mouth to mouth as if on wings. The children stayed indoors wherever he appeared, and if he rang at a door to ask for bread, the door remained shut. And although his pockets were full of gold, he had nothing to eat. Then he remembered his wife and children and went back to them, not because he loved them, but because he was hungry.

It was night by the time he reached his house. The children were sitting at the table and his wife was giving them their food. She ran to him and threw her arms round his neck. But he pushed her away.

"Don't you love me any more?" she asked softly.

"No," he said.

She came to him again and laid her head on his breast. Then she shrank back, for she felt the cold against her cheek.

"Then it is true," she whispered in horror. "I did not believe it."

"It is true," he said. "Send the children to bed, for I must eat."

The children went silently upstairs and the man without a heart sat down at the table and ate. When he had eaten he leaned forward in his chair and looked at her.

"Our troubles are over," he said. "We have money enough."

"Oh, yes," said his wife, "but you do not love me any more."

"That is true," said the man. "That was the price."

"What use is money," asked his wife, "if you can buy nothing for it?"

"The people will grow used to me," said the man, "and then their doors will open again."

"Oh, yes. But what you get will bring you no happiness. Come, look at your fine new son. He will warm your heart for you. There is something wonderful about him too: he has a birthmark like a flame over his own heart."

She picked up the seventh child from the cradle and held it before his eyes. The man felt no desire to see his seventh child.

"I do not care," he said. "But that was the price."

The child grew quickly—a boy named John. When he was nearly ten years old he heard from his brothers what had happened and began to think about it. He understood why the house was so quiet and why their father never gave them a good-night kiss when they went to bed.

And he understood why there was always plenty of food on the table, although his father never worked, but sat silently in his chair looking out of the window. He understood, too, why no visitors came and why everybody avoided the house. One day he even knew why there was a fiery red birthmark on his chest, for all that had happened just when he was born. And he took pity on his father and went to him.

"Father," he said, "is it true that you have no heart?"

"It is true," said his father. "But that was the price."

"Do you want to have it back again?" asked the boy.

His father looked at him in silence. "I want nothing," he said at last, "for I have no heart."

"Would you like me to bring it back?"

"I would like nothing," said his father. "How can I like anything?"

"The ten years are nearly over. You were promised that after ten years you could see the Devil again if you wished."

"How can I wish for anything?" said the father. "I sit here and wait for death. But do what your heart tells you. You still have one."

Then the boy prepared for a journey, for the day of his tenth birthday was approaching. He embraced his brothers and sisters and gave his mother a kiss. Then he went to his father and asked:

"Have you anything to tell me?"

"Nothing," said the man, "for I do not even remember your name."

"My name is John," said the boy. "Give me your hand, at least, for I have a difficult journey ahead of me."

"Why should I?" said his father. "Go along."

So John went out into the wide world in search of the Devil. He had only a little time left, for his birthday was the day after next, but many things can happen in two days.

On the evening of the first day he came to an inn. The people were friendly and wondered that so young a boy should be abroad quite alone. While his bed was being prepared upstairs he stayed down in the taproom eating his supper. He listened to what the other guests were saying and after a while the talk came round to a man who had changed greatly in the last ten years. Before that he had never spoken a word to a soul, but suddenly he had changed. He had become lively and talkative and above all he loved children, although he had none himself. Yet people did not trust him, for he lived quite alone. But what surprised people most was that he was rich and yet had never done a hand's turn of work. He sometimes went fishing, but only for pleasure.

"That must be the man who has my father's heart," thought the boy, and he asked where the man lived.

The innkeeper told him the way, but his wife shook her head.

"Do not go there, my child," she said anxiously. "You will find nothing good there."

But the boy, who was sure that his father's heart was there, replied: "I must go. And tomorrow is the last day."

"Then rise early," said the innkeeper, "because he is setting out on a journey tomorrow."

Then the boy knew for certain that he had found the one he sought, recalling that the Devil had said to his father: "After ten years you can summon me. If you want me, I will come. But you will not want me."

Now the Devil was setting out on a journey—could this mean that the fisherman *had* summoned him, after all? This thought gave the boy fresh courage.

Next morning he got up early, before the sun appeared in the sky. He ran through the darkness in the direction the man had shown him and saw an old woman coming towards him.

"So," said the woman, "you are an early bird! And where are you going?

"I am going to the Devil," said John.

The woman looked at him respectfully. *"You* can do that," she said, "for he is powerless over the innocent. Do you see the smoke in the distance? That is where he lives. But you must hurry, for he is going away. He does that every ten years, and today is the day."

The Devil himself opened the door when the boy knocked. He was fanning himself, as if he felt too hot.

"Come in," he said, "you are just in time, for I was going to visit someone. You look like him."

He led John to a great room, where there was a sound as if many clocks were ticking. The boy looked round and saw a hundred or more glass cases hanging against the walls. And in each of them hung a heart, still beating.

"A little hobby," said the Devil lightly. "Come and sit with me awhile: what can I do for you?"

The boy stood still and said: "You are the Devil."

Then the Devil sat down, for he suddenly knew that he had met his match.

"How do you know that?" he asked softly.

The boy's own heart was beating until it nearly choked him, but his voice was firm.

"I know it," he said, "and I want to know more. Whose are all those hearts?"

Now the Devil would never have answered this unless he had been feeling very weak himself. He was carrying the father's heart in his breast and he could not resist the child.

"Ask something else," he said.

"No. I am asking *that*."

The Devil struggled against a feeling he had never known before, and against which he was powerless.

"All right," he said, "people have sold their souls to me. Now go, for you know too much already."

"And why do you visit them after ten years?"

"I have to. If they want to, they can have their hearts back. But most of them do not. They have grown used to me. Go now, for you know too much already."

But the boy suddenly said: "Give me back my father's heart."

The Devil turned pale. "Ask for something else," he whispered.

"No. I am asking for that."

The Devil stared helplessly. The strange feeling was growing stronger and stronger and he could refuse the boy nothing. But suddenly he had an idea. He put his hand into his bosom, drew out the father's heart and laid it on the table. And in the same instant he drew a breath of relief, for once that heart was no longer in his breast, the child's power over him was broken. He stared at John with chilly eyes and said:

"No."

But the boy had already jumped up and seized the heart from the table. He ran as fast as he could, looking back constantly, for he thought the Devil was after him. But he was wrong about that, for the Devil had not the heart to follow him. He went on sitting where he was and could not stir hand or foot.

It was already evening when the boy rushed into his house. His father was sitting by the window.

"Father, father!" he cried breathlessly. "I have brought back your heart!"

The father looked at him indifferently, and shrugged his shoulders. Then he turned and looked out of the window, as he had been doing for ten years.

The boy was dumbfounded. But suddenly he realized that his father could not help his strange aloofness, because he was still possessed of the Devil. Quickly he pushed the heart, which he had been carrying in his hands all this time, into the man's bosom and in a twinkling everything had changed!

The fisherman stood up and clasped his son in his arms. Then he looked about him and for the first time in ten years he really saw his wife and children. The tears ran down his cheeks. "How big you have grown!" he cried. "And how I love you all." He saw the fire on the hearth and the kettle over the fire. He listened ecstatically to the wind in the chimney and the rain against the windowpanes. He heard the singing of the water boiling in the kettle and gazed in astonishment at a red geranium blooming on the window ledge. Everything was new to him and everything gave him joy. He kissed his wife on both cheeks and sat down at the table among his seven children.

"How I love you all!" he cried, again and again.

But he loved the youngest best of all, for the boy had truly stolen his heart away.

The Bird Witch

LONG ago there lived a king. He lived in a great palace of seventy-nine rooms. Really, there were eighty rooms, but there was one little room which no one ever entered. It was at the very top of a tower and the way to it was up an old, winding staircase. The steps were broken and tufts of grass and stinging nettles grew in the cracks. Fat spiders wove their webs from wall to wall and in the window corners sat fiery red toads. They puffed themselves up and hissed whenever they heard a footstep. No wonder that the king had expressly forbidden everyone to climb that staircase!

"Come, let us be sensible," he said. "There is nothing we want up there, and there are enough things to be seen in the world already."

Well, that was what he said, but at the top of the stairs was a little door and if you opened it, you were in the witch's room. She was a good woman, but she was very angry. Years ago, when the previous king was still alive, she had lived downstairs and eaten at the royal table. She had everything her own way: she had her own dish and on it were thistles, toadstools and pieces of bark. Nor would she eat with knife and fork, but stirred her food with her brown fingers and cut it with her long nails. Whenever she took a bite, a puff of white smoke came out of her mouth and when she had finished she said in her harsh voice: "Get up!" and then she flew three times round the table on her broomstick and rushed away.

The previous king had quite enjoyed all this. He liked the crusty old woman and understood that witches were not like other people. But his son thought otherwise and when he became king he drove the witch away.

"Out!" he said. "No smoking at meals."

Poor old witch! She stood up and sighed. And for the first time the puff of smoke that came out of her mouth was not white, but black. The young king was afraid, for the smoke was as black as soot and boded no good. But he had said what he had said and he could not take it back.

"I have been eating here for eighteen years," she said in her harsh voice, "and now I am not allowed to do so any more. You will regret it."

She took a ring from her finger, laid it on the edge of the table and flew away. The king picked up the ring and looked at it.

"Scrap iron," he said, and threw the ring out of the window.

That very year a daughter was born to him. The little girl grew fast and was as pretty as a picture. She had blue eyes, pink cheeks and a mouth like a cupid's bow. But the loveliest thing of all was her golden hair, which was like spun gold and rippled down to her waist. And when she was eighteen it reached to her feet and she could hide herself in it. And so she did. For the princess was ashamed. Right through her fair tresses ran a raven lock. It was a thick, dark strand, as black as soot. The court physician had tried to remove it and the court hairdresser had cut it off hundreds of times, but all in vain. In a few hours the coal-black hair grew again and streamed like a dark rivulet among the golden waves. And so the princess was ashamed, for no one wanted to marry her. There were princes enough, but when they saw the princess they were afraid.

"Where does that black hair come from?" they asked. "Is she bewitched?"

Of course, the princess was bewitched, but no one knew that for certain. And the princess knew nothing about it at all, because she had never heard of the witch.

But one evening a bird flew into her room. It was coal-black, with sharp quills instead of feathers, and its brown claws had long talons.

When the princess picked it up, it gave a harsh cry and pecked at her hand. But she saw that it was sick so she took care of it. For two weeks she carried it about with her in the warmth of her rippling hair, until the poor little bird grew real feathers. Its harsh cries faded and it began to sing. Its ugly claws vanished, too, and fine little feet grew instead. But it was not cured. And when two weeks had passed, it laid its head on one side and died.

The princess took the bird, wrapped it in her best embroidered handkerchief, and buried it in the garden. She dug up the soil with her own hands and laid the small body in the warm ground. As she was covering it, she found in the earth the iron ring which her father had thrown away. She put it on her finger and at once all the birds in the garden began to sing.

And this was what they sang:

> "Maiden with the golden hair
> What if there are eighty there?"

The princess did not understand this, for she had far more than eighty hairs on her head. But then she thought of the seventy-nine rooms in the palace and set out in search of the eightieth. She found the old spiral staircase and climbed it fearlessly. The stinging nettles between the stones stung her and the fiery red toads puffed themselves up and hissed. But the princess climbed bravely on and came to an oak door fastened with seven bolts. She shot back the bolts one by one and every bolt gave a loud sigh. Then she opened the door and saw an old woman sitting there.

"Well, well," said the witch, putting her glasses into her spectacle case, "so this is the king's daughter. I have been expecting you, my child. You were good to me, for I was the black bird."

How strange! Her harsh voice had gone and she spoke softly and tenderly. The old woman went on:

"For eighteen years I have been angry. But you have taught me to sing again and stroked my feathers to life. So I will take away the curse which your father brought upon you."

She stood up and stroked the princess's golden hair. The crone's long nails had vanished and her hands were as soft as rose petals. And as she stroked, the black tress fell to the ground. It coiled its way across the floor and hissed, as the toads on the staircase did, and slipped away through a crack in the wood. The old woman put a red rose in the princess's hair and kissed her on the mouth. And in that very instant she vanished.

The princess married very soon afterwards. From eighty princes she chose the handsomest and, when he became king in his own country, she was his queen. And on the grave of the dead bird red roses bloomed all summer and all winter long. The gardener was astonished, but the queen said nothing. One need not always tell all one knows.

The Sunday Child

ONCE upon a time there were a father and mother who had six children. Each child was born on a different day of the week. The eldest child was called Monday and the youngest Saturday. And the rest were called after the days in between.

But they had no Sunday child, and that was just what the father and mother longed for most. They were very pleased with the six that they had, but they were more concerned about the one child they lacked. They went sorrowfully about the house, glancing at the empty stool that always stood ready. And every time they sat down to meals they pulled the baby's cradle up to the table, for you never know.

The old grandmother heard about this. She was only a tiny person, with a pleated bonnet, a piping voice and a hump on her back. Her right leg was a little shorter than the other, too, although she herself insisted that it was her left leg that was a little longer.

But she could make spells. In former times she had made spells all day, but now she did it only in the evening after dinner and it made her very tired.

"Relax, little lady," the doctor had said. "Just a few little tricks, and we will be all right." But she could not stop, and would perform the big spells, too. Fortunately, for otherwise the Sunday child never would have arrived. As we shall see now.

On a certain day the old grandmother came to stay with the family for a week. This happened every year and now the time had come again. She clambered up the stairs to her room under the roof and at once started to study a thick book.

"Don't bother about me," she said in her piping voice. "I've got all my sandwiches with me. And when the week is over I will come down on my own."

She did not sleep, she did not drink and she did not make spells, but just kept on reading all week long. Every day one of the six children—the one born on that day—came up with a cup of tea, but she did not take the cup. "Just put it down by the other cups," she said. By Sunday there were six cups standing in a row, and then she came down.

"It has taken a long time," she piped, "for the letters were so small and it was right at the back of the book. But now I know how to do it. Listen, little mother, I will tell you. You must look at sunflowers for nine months. If you keep it up, the child will come as sure as eggs!"

And she climbed onto her broomstick, circled the room and flew quickly out of the window.

The father thought it was a lot of nonsense, but since sunflower seed cost only a penny a tin, "Nothing venture, nothing win!" he said to himself, and bought a pennyworth of sunflowers. He sowed the seeds in the garden and in the flowerpots which stood on the piano. And he himself filled the bedroom washbasins with earth and put the sunflower seeds in them. For the more he thought about it, the more he felt there was something in it. And in any case he did not like washing.

The sunflowers bloomed splendidly. First the ones on the piano, then the ones in the washbasins and finally those in the garden, too. They waved their great golden heads in the sun and the mother looked at them all day, full of hope.

And it happened just as the old grandmother had foretold. One evening, when the nine months had passed, they sat down at the table and the Sunday child was lying in the cradle. It was a Sunday evening and you could easily see that it was a Sunday child, for it had fiery red hair and freckles. And it was such a sunny soul that the father quickly put out the best golden gingerbread biscuits and washed himself all over for the first time in nine months. He also picked a great bunch of sunflowers and went over to the old grandmother, to thank her once again.

But the grandmother was sitting in her armchair, looking very wretched.

"John, John," she piped miserably, "we have made a great mistake. We should have read it all the way through."

She pushed the book across the table to him and pointed with her finger at the last page. The father was startled. For this was what he read: "Here ends our little book. And we repeat once again: Good people, take care, for these Sunday children have one drawback: they grow terribly large. So think what you are doing. The End. Copyright reserved."

After that the father kept looking to see if it was true. And indeed it was. The child already weighed twelve pounds and was nearly growing out of the cradle. He hadn't noticed at first, but now it was obvious. And the boy was so strong that he could even push his rattle out through the wickerwork. And that was not all. After a year he was so enormous that he had to sit in his father's chair and was not allowed to touch anything, for he broke everything to pieces. And after two years no one dared to play with the Sunday child any more, he had grown so strong. The father kept it up the longest, but when he had had his arm broken twice, he took to going out for a walk on Sundays and always looked through the window before going in again.

When the boy was four years old he carried his mother on his arm when she took him to school in the morning. And after another year he was rolling a wagon wheel for a hoop and playing with cannon balls. When he flew a kite the sun was blotted out in the sky, the kite was so huge. That was the only time that anyone saw the child cry, for he adored the sun and could not bear to miss a moment of daylight. The boy could look straight at the sun hour after hour without blinking, and on one else could do that.

The Sunday child grew and grew. At school his head was already above the roof and the teacher had to climb up a ladder to hear his lesson. When it was time to eat, two carts stood ready, one holding his bread and butter and the other carrying what was to go on it. When he went to the circus he had to crawl in on his hands and knees and once, when he got up too soon because he thought the show was already over, the tent hung like a collar round his neck.

But the worst was still to come. When he was eighteen no girl would have him — no girl could hear what he was saying. His head was above the clouds and, however hard he tried, all anyone heard was a distant rumble in the heavens, as if a storm were about to break.

Finally the Sunday child realized that there was no place for him in this world. He waded through the sea until he came to a high mountain. He stepped onto the mountain and waited until the sun was passing. Then he stretched up his arms, tensed his muscles, and made a mighty leap that landed him in the middle of the sun.

Soft green grass grew there, every blade as tall as ten houses, and

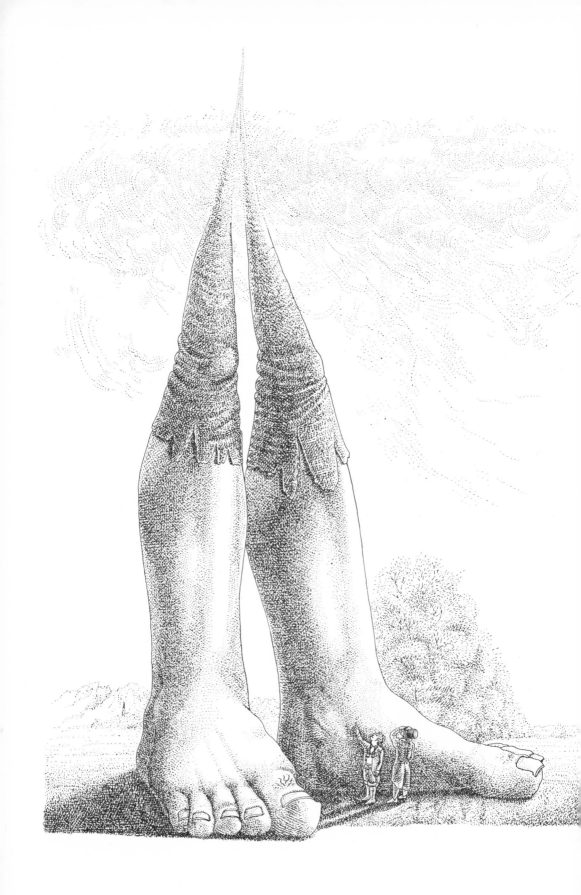

in the fields bloomed the sunflowers. They were not called sunflowers there, but buttercups, because the people there were far bigger than on earth and regarded sunflowers as little plants. To them the Sunday child did not seem large at all, but just the right size. So he married the daughter of a Sunday school teacher who had nothing to do during the week. The Sunday child soon took over the school and gave the Sunday lessons there. All the other days he rested with his bride in the long yellow corn and thought of his weekday brothers whose lives were so much harder than his. Then he would jump up, seize his wife round the waist and sing:

> "I am a Sunday child, hooray!
> But I am glad all week as well,
> For I have six whole days for play—
> On Sunday rings the lesson bell.
> Oh, sweetheart mine, what joy for me,
> A sunny Sunday child to be!"

Everyone on the sun found the words so suitable, yet so profound, that they were set to music and eagerly learned by heart.

And if you are sitting in the sunshine on a summer's day, when it is quite still and even the sparrows are silent, listen hard. Then, far away in the distance, you will hear them singing, if you put your hand to your ear and do not stir an eyelash. And if you can sing, then sing it with them.

A White
Christmas

ONCE upon a time there was a man who wanted to celebrate Christmas properly. He took a little ladder from the barn and hung all over the ceiling the red paper chains which prove that it's Christmastime. From the lamp he hung one of those red bells which don't look much when they are folded up but are quite appealing afterwards. Then he laid the table. He had stood in line for hours in three separate shops, but at least the results were good.

By each place he put a candle, one of those you buy ten to a box, and then he clapped his hands. That was the signal to come in. His wife and children, who had been standing in the kitchen all that time, glancing at each other with embarrassed smiles, came in, quite bewildered.

"Oh," they cried, "you should not have done that."

But since he had done it, they sat down and looked at each other warmly.

"And now we are not simply going to stuff ourselves," said the man, "we must also think about what it was that actually happened."

He read aloud the story of Mary and Joseph going from one inn to another, unable to find room anywhere. But the child was born at last, albeit in a stable.

Then they began to eat, because this was the right time, even if there was a great deal of hardship in the world.

"There," said the man, "this is how to celebrate Christmas, this is how it should be," and he was right.

And they were amazed at the hardheartedness of all the innkeepers, but after all, it was two thousand years ago, remember; that kind of thing does not happen now.

At that moment there was a ring at the door. The man irritably laid down the party fork he was just raising to his lips.

"That *is* tiresome," he said. "Something always has to happen."

He took off his napkin, brushed the crumbs from his knees and strolled to the front door. On the step stood a man with a beard and bright, pale eyes. He asked if he could take shelter, because it was snowing hard. (Actually, it was a White Christmas. I forget to say that, how could I have been so silly?) The two men looked at each other in silence for a moment and then the first man was seized by a great anger.

"On Christmas Day, too!" he said. "Aren't there any other evenings?" and he slammed the door behind him.

But in the dining room a strange feeling came over him and the turkey no longer tasted so good.

"I'm just going to have a look," he said. "Something has happened, but I don't know what."

He went back to the front door and looked out through the swirling snow. He was just in time to see the man disappearing round the corner with a young woman beside him who was with child. He ran to the corner and stared up the street, but there was no one to be seen. The two of them seemed to have dissolved in the snow. For it was, as I have said, a White Christmas.

When he returned to the dining room he was pale and there were tears in his eyes.

"Don't say anything," he said. "The wind's a bit sharp, but it will soon pass."

And it was quite true, you do have to get over things. It was a very nice Christmas party, they hadn't had a real one like this for years. It went on snowing all night, and once again the child was born in a stable.

The Three Wise Men

LONG ago there lived a very rich man. He had everything he could think of and so he thought little. Every day he lay on the balcony of his house and looked happily round at all his possessions. He had an exquisite wife who adored him and she was expecting their first child. When she was walking in the garden she would look up and smile at him. And he would nod back and think: "She is mine." He looked at the cattle grazing in the valleys round his house, and at his barns which were full of figs and dates and lemons. And again he thought: "All this is mine." And he looked at the donkey carts laden with grapes making their way slowly to the hill where his house stood, and once again he thought: "They too belong to me."

One night as he lay on his back gazing at the sky, he noticed an especially large star. It stood low on the horizon, yet it shone more brightly than the other stars. The rich man sat upright and for the first time for years he had a new thought. He rang for his servant and said:

"Fetch the wise man. I have had a new thought."

The servant ran off joyfully to fetch the wise man who worked for his master. He had had nothing to do for three years, as that was the last time a question had been put to him, and he had not known the answer to that one. Yet he slept in the next room in order to be near at hand and he was at his master's bedside in a moment.

"You sent for me?"

"Certainly. I have had a new thought."

The wise man clasped his hands.

"It is this. Not everything is mine."

The wise man looked about him in astonishment, for as far as the eye could see, the land belonged to his master.

"Idiot," said the latter, "look up!" For the star had risen meanwhile and was now right above their heads.

"This is no star," said the wise man. "It is a comet. And comets bring happiness."

"Good. And here is my question: what is happiness?"

The wise man had given much thought to this question, for his room was small and the food was bad. He had reached the conclusion that happiness lived in the next room, but he dared not say so. So he was silent and looked at the woman in the garden, for he had no wife.

"You do not know," said the rich man.

"I only know," said the wise man, "that you are happy."

"You call yourself a wise man," said the rich man scornfully, "and you don't even know that the happy lack nothing. The stars are mine. They stand immovable above my head and they belong to me. I can count them. But a comet moves. Tomorrow it belongs to someone else. Well now, happiness is a perfect thing. If it lacks anything, it is not happiness. So I am not happy, and that is my new thought."

The wise man did not know an answer to this; the rich man, being frugal, had not hired the best wise man.

"Fetch three more wise men," said the rich man, "so that when my son is born he will know that he is truly happy."

On that very day three wise men had come into town. The rich man had a sack of dates taken to each of them. The wise men distributed the dates to the poor but kept the sacks, thinking that they might come in handy.

"I want to be truly happy," said the rich man.

The wise men nodded, for they knew this already.

"Which is the wisest of you?" asked the rich man.

"The wisest is he who thinks he knows least."

"Which of you knows least?"

All three wise men stepped forward together.

"This will get us nowhere," said the rich man. "Let the other two wait in the next room; the third stays here."

Two of them bowed and went away. The rich man spoke to the remaining wise man:

"How can I find happiness?"

"By not looking for it," said the wise man.

The rich man thought about this, but he did not understand it.

"Then what *is* happiness?" he asked.

"Happiness," replied the wise man, "is giving in to something else."

"Can I recognize it?"

"We recognize it when it is past."

"This is no good to me at all," said the rich man. "Go and call the second."

The first wise man bowed and the second came in.

"How can I be happy?" asked the rich man.

"By expecting nothing," said the wise man.

"Are *you* happy?"

"If I knew that I would no longer be it."

"Where is happiness?"

"Happiness is where one is not."

"Very profound," said the rich man, "but it does not help me. Go and fetch the third."

The second wise man bowed and the third came in.

"Who finds happiness?" asked the rich man.

"He who has no need of it," said the wise man.

"What am I, when all my wishes are fulfilled?"

"A man without desire."

"Is that happiness?"

"No. It is satisfaction."

"Extraordinary," said the rich man, "and now, go."

And the third man bowed, too, and went.

The rich man spent a few moments thinking over everything he had heard, since he had paid for it with plentiful sacks of dates and the date harvest had been poor that year. Then he went out for some fresh air. And at his door he found the three wise men. They were sitting on the steps, holding their cloth sacks wide open before them. The passers-by were throwing in money, and when there was enough to keep them from hunger that day, they stood up and bought a few dates. The rich man watched them eating and said:

"It is a warm evening. I would like to stay with you for a little."

"Then eat with us," said the wise men.

The rich man sat down with them and shared their meal. A soft wind was blowing and over their heads sparkled thousands of stars. They were not moving, and even that one star stood still. This filled the rich man with great joy.

"I am almost happy now," he said, "but not quite. The star will certainly begin to move again. Can you not stay here? Then I would be content."

The three wise men were silent, as if they were waiting for something.

"I understand," said the rich man quickly. "I will make each of you a present."

"We need nothing," said the wise men.

"I know," said the rich man, "you will just give it to the poor. These will be presents meant for you alone."

He clapped his hands and said to his servant: "Bring three gifts here, but they must be something special."

The servant brought three packets and each wise man received one. They did not open them, yet their eyes shone with joy.

"Because you have given *this*," said the oldest of them, who was also the darkest, "you may go with us. For this is just what we were waiting for."

The rich man's face clouded over. "*Go* with you?" he cried, "but you are staying *here*!"

"Impossible."

"Why?"

"Because we must follow the star. It is standing still now and so we are resting. But as soon as it moves we will travel on. Come with us."

"Running after a star?" cried the rich man. "Leaving house and home?"

"We did that, too," said one of the three, "and we had more than you."

"Never."

"Think," said the wise man urgently, "for your wish is almost fulfilled."

But the rich man went in and closed the door behind him. Before going to bed he stood by the window again and looked up. The star had gone.

"What did you give the men?" he asked his servant.

The man stood up respectfully. "A lump of gold," he replied, "a pot of frankincense and a strange aromatic gum which is called myrrh."

Somewhere deep within the house came the cry of a child.

"What is that?"

"A son. Your first-born."

The rich man shivered, for the night had grown chill.

The Angel

ON the top of the Christmas tree stood an angel. How she got there she could not, with the best will in the world, remember. She retained a vague memory of a narrow, dark place from which she had been lifted by a small hand into a sea of light. It had been a glorious moment, and since that moment she had always been happy. That "always" had been a single evening, but for an angel on a Christmas tree that is eternity, as you may know. Poor little Christmas tree angel! She did not know that Christmas lasts only a day and that day was nearly over.

There she stood, fixed to the tree with a metal clip, swaying gently to and fro and looking through her gauzy wings at the light of the candles burning beneath her.

Suddenly one of the candles went out. Another followed. It was getting darker and darker, and in the end she could see nothing but the darkness of night. The angel sneezed, because the smell of the snuffed candles tickled her nose. To begin with she thought it was a joke, but when it was dark she began to think.

"I ought to have paid more attention when it was light," she thought regretfully, "I didn't look at all. I remember nothing. Absolutely nothing. If only it were light again!"

And it was light. But how different this light was! Pale, dingy and reluctant, it entered through a big square window, and before it had reached full strength a servant came into the room, picked up the Christmas tree and took it up to the attic. Bang! There lay the angel, looking straight into a crack in the plank floor.

It was terribly cold and unusually cheerless. At first the angel thought again: "Come, come, it's just a joke," but when she had been looking through the crack in the wooden floor for three whole days and nights, she began to be seriously worried And the longer she thought

181

of the light from the square window, the more clearly she understood that *light* was the most beautiful thing she had ever seen.

"I will try to explain it to you," she said one March day to a mouse who was just passing by. "Through a glass gap in the sky a blinding light fell on my head. That is the most beautiful thing I have ever seen. I cannot tell you how happy I was. But I was foolish in those days: I did not know. Now I do know and it is too late. But at least I have the memory."

"That's always something," said the mouse, after he had thought it over for a time. "Goodbye, I must be going."

One day a maid came into the attic and found the Christmas angel lying on the floor in her dusty corner. She picked her up and threw her in the coal hole. There she lay between two peat squares, directly opposite a gloomy looking piece of anthracite. The angel kept quiet for a week, because she did not find the company fit to talk to. But at last, one day in September, she could restrain herself no longer.

"You have not the faintest idea," she said, "what the light in the attic is like. It almost hurts your eyes, it is so dazzling. Sadly enough, I was too limited then to grasp my blessed state fully. But at least I have something to remember now."

"That is always something," said the piece of anthracite, "but I find the light in here quite reasonable."

The angel was silent. It was useless to argue with such a narrow-minded outlook.

Now, one morning the little boy who lived in the house was playing in the coal hole. Seeing the angel there, he picked it up and threw it in the rubbish bin. In there, it was pitch-black. At first the angel regarded her new state as a joke, but when it had been dark for three days, so dark that no one in the dustbin could have seen his hand before his eyes, she began to think. She thought and she thought and at last she could not contain herself and cried:

"Is there anyone here to listen to me?"

"Oh yes," said a fragment of mirror glass, "if it's not soo silly."

And the angel spoke of the blinding light in the coal hole and how thrilling it had been there.

"I was too stupid," she finished with a sigh, "to understand it, but I understand it now. I can see the whole thing!"

The fragment of glass was silent, because it had seen so much vanity in its life that it had become somewhat shy.

One afternoon when it was already dusk the trash man arrived. He took the lid off the bin and saw the angel lying there. Now it is always nice to find an angel, but if you are a trash man it makes you

doubly happy. He put the angel in his pocket and gave it to his wife that evening.

"There you are," he said, "for the Christmas tree."

And the trash man's wife hid the angel in a cardboard box and put the box in a cupboard.

"Hallo," said the angel, after having lain there in silence for a while, "is there anyone there?"

But there was nothing in the box but the shavings in which the angel lay; and shavings, as you know, are quiet by nature. And that was quite all right, because the angel really had nothing to tell. However much she thought and pondered over her old dustbin, she could not see anything more in it than in the cardboard box she was lying in now: both had been equally dark. Finally, when she realized that it could be no darker, she let the past go and thought about the future. A new feeling filled her; she felt happy and full of expectancy. All regrets and all bitterness melted from her heart and she lay still, waiting with open eyes for the little hand which would lift her up out of the darkness to the light.

And then the hand came and lifted her up to the top of the Christmas tree. The Christmas tree was much smaller than the year before and there were fewer lights on it, but the angel did not notice. Fastened to the top with a metal clip, she rocked gently to and fro and looked through her gauzy wings at the sparkling decorations on the tree.

"Delightful," she thought, "delightful. This time I must be sure to pay attention. It will soon be over. And then I will have seen and known everything."

She kept her eyes wide open and stared straight down through the twigs. There she saw the trash man in his new suit, his wife and their little girl, with a blue ribbon in her hair. And the eyes of the child were looking directly into a small, open room in which there were also a man, a woman and a child, but much, much smaller, and also an ox and an ass, as big as the animals in a toybox. Suddenly the angel started, for there on the roof of the house was fixed an angel like herself, with the same gauzy wings and holding in her hands a ribbon the same as she herself was holding. For the first time she could read the words written on it: "Glory to God and Peace on Earth to Men of Good Will."

At the top of the tree, a feeling of profound joy filled the lonely angel, who had so long considered herself abandoned and wronged.

"I have a Message in my hands," she thought proudly. "Now nothing more can touch me. Whatever misfortunes befall me, I have my treasure with me and no one can take it away."

And many misfortunes befell her, for in the fourth year she broke away from the tree and landed in a box of bricks and from there she got into the ragbag. At last she was lying in the garden on a heap of dry leaves, looking up at the hurrying clouds. She could feel herself slowly and painlessly disintegrating day by day, but she held on firmly to her ribbon and there was no bitterness in her.

For she knew that she was a creature doomed to die, but chosen to preserve the Good News to the end.

The Twelfth King

YOUR mother can't do it. No, even your grandmother can't do it. No one can tell you *this* story, because it is too long. It began in very ancient times and it is still going on.

So, in order to distinguish it from other stories, this one is often referred to as The Story. Your mother and your grandmother can certainly tell you who the Man is that made it, so I will not name Him. It would be better for you to hear His name from your mother than from me. But in this story, which is part of The Story, I shall refer to Him by a strange name: The Twelfth King.

He won't appear until the end of this tale, just as He will only appear when The Story has already happened.

Once upon a time there lived in a great, dark palace, where the wind whined along the walls at night, a king, a real one. His beard was like a pillar and his voice was like thunder. A king needs no more. His name was Teuton and people also sometimes called him Germania. Wherever he went, his subjects lay down in the dust and if they did not lie down they were knocked down, so you can see how powerful the king was.

Now this king had a son, Democratio. And this son had a hollow head. His head really *was* hollow. There was nothing in it, nothing at all. It is difficult for us to believe this, because our heads are full. Of course if they were not, it would be still more difficult.

In the beginning the prince was unaware of this peculiarity, for in the first place he could not know that his head was hollow, because it was hollow. And in the second place no one could tell him, because you cannot see from the outside whether a head is hollow or not. And that is a good thing. Finally, no one would have dared to tell him, because it is not wise to tell a king's son the truth, unless it is pleasant.

But on his twentieth birthday, he was tearing downstairs when he hit his head against a beam. It gave out the sonorous ring of an empty champagne glass. The prince stood still in amazement. He tapped his head: it rang a high, light note.

"What's this," said the prince, surprised. "Can my head, this precious head of state, be empty?" He hastened to see the court physician.

Now the court physician was a wise man. He was sitting bowed over his books when the king's son came in.

"Examine this head," said the prince curtly.

And the physician, the wise man, did so. Now it is difficult to tell the truth about a princely head and keep your own at the same time. But the court physician was a wise man. He tapped the precious head with his silver hammer and listened carefully to the splendid ring of it.

"Sire," he said joyfully, "I congratulate you, it *is* hollow."

"Really?" cried the king's son, feeling suddenly happy. "Is it really hollow?"

The physician, the wise man, bowed.

"It is certainly most rare, sire," he said, "and that sublime ringing tone, too!"

"But," cried the king's son, "when my wicked father dies I shall have to reign. How can I reign with an empty head?"

Then the court physician tiptoed to the door and bolted it. He approached the princely ear and whispered, his shrewd eyes glittering:

"You have a splendid head to rule with. When there is any conflict in the land, this is what you do: first listen to one party and send him away."

"Oh yes," said the prince.

"Then listen to the other party and send him away."

"Oh yes," said the prince.

"Well," said the court physician, smiling, "that's all."

"But," asked the prince, "which party will be right?"

The court physician glanced around and listened. Then he leaned forward quickly: "The biggest," he said.

The old king was dead. The bells rang out and it was a day of rejoicing. And the new king mounted the throne with leaden feet. However, he reigned to the satisfaction of almost everyone, and the fame of his wisdom flew across the frontiers. And the secret of the hollow head remained in that head; you see how easy it is to hide nothing.

One day the king gave a great dinner. It is not easy to give you a picture of that dinner. It was so amazingly splendid that even the oldest of the servants trembled in their shoes.

Shimmering gentlemen and sparkling ladies sat at twelve long tables in the great hall. Behind each chair stood a footman, from whose features years of training had banished all emotion. Music was playing, so softly that it was almost inaudible; on the other hand, one would have noticed if it had not been there. But it was there, thank goodness. People spoke and ate very little. Although the most extraordinary dishes were present in abundance, they did not eat very much. And the little they did eat was lifted to their mouths with elegant grace and swallowed down with a gentle smile. In short, it was what the members of the upper classes call a successful evening. The king himself was in a state of restrained rapture. He pinched himself secretly on the thigh and turned his lovely empty head wherever it ought to be turned. The conversations were soft, and unimportant, and everything was as it ought to be.

Then, by chance, the king raised his head, lifted his eyes from his plate and looked down the hall. His gaze became suddenly stern: between the open double doors stood a dirty, sweaty man, gasping for breath.

"I say," cried the king, waving his fork, "what's this?"

"Lord, lord . . ."

"What?" said the king, rising from his chair.

The man shook.

"Sire," he said, "the crisis has come upon the land."

"The what?" asked the king.

"The crisis, lord . . ."

"Well," said the king, "that is awkward."

He had no idea what a crisis was, but he suspected it was something bad, so he looked as a king could be expected to look. His companions looked solemn too.

"Well, well," said the king, "now isn't that tiresome?"

He sat down again slowly and fiddled with his plate, but in his heart a great anxiety was growing.

Next morning the king awakened in his silken bed of state. He opened his eyes, slowly, raised them to the satin canopy and thought about the crisis. It was a pity that it should have come now. He had been getting on so nicely with his hollow head. First he must find out what a crisis actually was. What was the crisis? The king dressed himself quickly and summoned the wisest in the land. They came. Surrounded by the respectful people, they strode through the streets to the palace, step by step, their long beards thrown over their shoulders, sighing with wisdom. The head of one wise man was so heavy with all that was in it that it waggled on his thin neck. You can imagine what an impression it made.

They told the king what the crisis was. They took three hours over it and yet after only a few minutes the king's eyes were full of tears, for his heart was good and tender. He listened respectfully for three hours and then the wise men were silent.

The king sat crumpled on his throne, his face hidden in his hands. He was trembling. . . .

"Have you finished?" he asked in a low voice.

"Yes, sire," said the wise men, "that's it."

They combed their beards smooth and left and the king sat on his throne, alone. In the great, empty hall the evening began to fall, the late light dawdled through the windows and it grew dark. And the king sat there, alone on his throne, bowed and grieving, a small, sad figure. So ended the day.

Now the country was in an uproar and an answer had to be found. First of all a Royal Decree was issued ordering books to be written about the crisis by anyone who could hold a pen. And there were plenty of them. The book did not have to be exactly true, as long as it was thick and cheap. Then meetings had to be held, many meetings. There had to be at least two speakers and also an introduction, a postscript, a vote of thanks, and if there was any time left over, a word of honest tribute.

His subjects went to work with high hearts. As far as the books were concerned, the citizens divided themselves into two rival parties: those who wrote and those who read. But most time was allotted to the meetings. Evening after evening the subjects sat patiently listening, clapping their hands and putting sensible questions.

The king himself worked hardest of all. He did nothing but read what had been written from early morning to late at night. And he did it in his pajamas because there was naturally no time to get dressed. Once in a while he did have to get up to blow his nose, but then he read even faster to make up for lost time. He learned what money was and who had it, who did not have it and who ought to have it. He learned what workers were and what they looked like. He learned about the great laws of supply and demand, prices and values, and gradually his empty head filled up, growing heavier and heavier until one day it was completely full.

"And now," said the king, getting up gladly, "we must put all this knowledge to good use."

Then the laws began to fly over the land. Good laws, sensible laws, noble laws. But, all of you who may be reading this, now came the strangest thing of all: the crisis went on. Famine increased in the land, the subjects became impatient, the new king no longer seemed as wise as they had thought him. When this came to the king's ears, he smiled sadly and he devised new laws, good laws, sensible laws, noble laws. And the famine continued to increase.

There was a lot of grey in the king's beard now. He lay awake for nights in his silken bed, his eyes wide open, his hands plucking at the sheets. Then, one night, he sat up suddenly. He laid his index finger against his royal nose and smiled. His eyes shone. Then he slipped down again and fell peacefully asleep.

Next morning the couriers raced across the frontiers on foaming horses. They blew cheerfully on their copper horns, or clacked their tongues. For now an answer had been found! Ten kings were needed, ten powerful kings, to put everything to rights in one meeting. In every country the flags flew from the windows and the people ran down the streets to see the kings arriving. There they came: the king of Baroba, the king of Bonuri, the king of the Land of Sir, the king of Piroga, the kings of Jerba, Bano and Jaffi, the king of Jap, the king of Bacco and the king of the Land of Tassa. By the way, I should tell you that the king of Rome did not come. His territory was too small and they could get on quite well without him.

So the famous Eleven Kings Conference began. After appearing on the balcony to be cheered by the crowd, they withdrew for their councils. Each king had brought an army of chroniclers, scholars and private secretaries, who formed a great, scribbling body, which gradually split up into committees, main committees, special committees and sub-committees, which branched off into advisory bodies and legal working parties; and then it was evening. King Democratio uttered a few soothing words to the people from the balcony and they all went to bed. Next morning the eleven kings, the chroniclers, the scholars and the private secretaries dressed quickly, ate quickly and branched out again. So it went on for many days, until in the end the network of committees was stretched so fine that it could not be spun out any further. Meanwhile King Democratio had grown tired of soothing the people from the balcony every evening, and special people had been appointed to distribute across the land papers on which the soothing words were printed.

But although the eleven kings worked hard and although the papers rejoiced, the crisis remained.

The king no longer slept at all. The people saw his snow-white beard everywhere: he conferred with the chairman of the sub-sections of the sub-committees, he reminded the men who wrote the papers of their responsible task, he sat at the head of the eleven kings' dinners and, taxing his powers to the utmost, he spoke vigorously about the conclusions of the conference and steps to be taken in the right direction. His eyes were deep and sad, his hands white and shaking. And the people began to murmur, softly and secretly, like an irritated beast. They had expected bread and they were getting paper, they said—and other such strange sayings. One evening they assembled under the balcony, with pale, drawn faces, in silence. The soldiers came and chased them away but the following evening they came back. The soldiers came, and they stayed there too: they were trampled underfoot. And from all the streets people appeared, more and more people, an uncountable multitude. They shouted for the kings. They wanted to see the kings! There was a single howl of voices, one enormous, raging sound, and the eleven kings appeared on the balcony.

Thousands of fists flew up and an indescribable roar arose. The eleven kings stood there with bowed heads, eleven simple fools. They tried to speak, but no one heard them. They begged for silence, but no one listened. Then one high, furious voice arose from the people: "There is still one king who has not been called!" Prince Democratio leaned over the balustrade: "Who is that, then," he asked mockingly. There was a sudden silence.

Then the same voice cried: "You eleven kings—eleven purple fools, fools of wisdom and understanding—who gave you the crowns on your heads and the ermine on your shoulders?" And the eleven kings were silent.

That single voice had spoken well. We would be powerless with eleven kings, if the Twelfth were forgotten. But, you will say, two thousand years ago, on Whit Sunday, was not the world saved by eleven men meeting together? And they were fishermen and had nothing but their bare hands? But *they* never forgot the King!

The Chest
and the
Student

ONCE upon a time there lived a student who did not believe in ghosts or magicians. "Nonsense," said he. "I have never met one, so they do not exist."

Now that was a very strange argument and as we shall see, he was wrong.

The student lived in a very remarkable street called Pinker Street. On one side of the street the houses were fine and stately, but on the other side they were dirty and dilapidated. That was where most of the people lived. There was a little boy living there too, who lay in bed all day long, coughing. He had waved to the student once or twice, but the student never waved back. He was always studying. Only in the evening he would smoke a pipe by the window, looking straight into the narrow, over-filled rooms on the other side. He had his thoughts to think and they were mostly pleasant thoughts. But there were times when they were less pleasant. Then he would light up a fresh pipe and chase them away in the smoke.

One evening the student came home late and found a long, black box on his table, with a white cross on the lid. "Curious," said the student. He opened the chest and found a note inside. This is what it said:

Dear Student,
At half past twelve tonight I shall be paying a call on you.
There is no need to be afraid. What do you think of this chest?
                    Yours sincerely,
                    A good thought.

"A good thought," repeated the student, "that's odd."
He called the landlord who lived on the floor below and asked:
"Tell me, landlord, has anyone been to my room?"

193

"No one, sir," said the landlord.

"Do you know anyone called 'a good thought'?"

"Not that I can think of, sir," said the landlord, "and I've never met one, either." And that was true.

"Then how did this chest get on my table?" asked the student.

The landlord took the chest in his hands and looked at it inside and out. Then he read the note.

"I'm going down to close the shutters at the windows, sir," he said, "and bolt the front door. I'm glad I'm not in your shoes."

The student laughed. "Just go down again, my dear fellow," he said, "this is all rubbish and silliness." He put on his slippers and sat down to read a learned book.

When the clock struck twelve he stood up and opened the window. There was no one to be seen in the street. The moon was shining on the house opposite and there were thousands of stars in the sky.

"A beautiful night," murmured the student, "but how few people know of it! How is it, then, that I can see it? Am I better than others? No. But I have the time for it; the others have to toil and moil the livelong day and by evening they are too tired to look upward to God's wide heaven. The world is upside down."

The clock struck half past twelve. It was a heavy stroke, which sounded over the roof tops, but the student paid no attention. He continued:

"Everyone makes plans to improve the world, but the world gets no better. It would be best for me to give away all the left-over money that I save, and never spend, to the family in the house opposite here. Perhaps the pale little lad would get better then. And if my neighbor did the same with the house opposite him, and so on, right down the street, then Pinker Street would be a happy place. And if all the streets all over the world did it, perhaps the whole world would be better. You have to begin someplace. Let this be the place."

"Very good," said a voice behind him in the room.

The student turned and saw someone sitting in his chair. The visitor was completely transparent, but he was dressed like an ordinary man. His hair was grey but his face was youthful and unwrinkled. He had a small, bullet-shaped head.

"Hello, who are you?" asked the student.

"I am a thought," said the little man, "and quite a good one, too. There are other kinds as well, but there have been enough of those here."

"Have you been here long?" asked the student.

"A few minutes. I was inside your head. And now I'm sitting here."

"Did I call you or something?" asked the student, crossly. "How did you get here?"

"I come and go," said the little man. "There is nothing you can do about it."

"Well, I should go, if I were you," said the student. "This is private property. I want to live alone and in peace."

"Those are just the kinds of rooms I like visiting," said the little man. "In any case, I will only stay a quarter of an hour. We never stay long. You're doing very nicely here. Only the view is a bit—how shall I put it?"

"Listen!" cried the student. "I don't want any part of this. And I don't believe in ghosts and magicians."

"But you'll have to believe in me," said his visitor, "because here I sit. You can't doubt that."

"I do doubt it," said the student. "It's all rubbish and silliness. I want to be alone and left in peace."

"What proof must I give of my presence?" asked the little man, placing his hat on his knees and gazing thoughtfully into the crown.

"There's an old chest behind you," said the student. "It has annoyed me for years. I can't very well throw it away, because it belonged to an old aunt of mine who imagined that I liked it. Can you turn it into something else?"

"It has already happened," said the visitor, without looking up.

The student looked at the chest. Then something quite extraordinary happened. The chest did not change; it stayed as it had been. But the student suddenly began to like it. He realized that the scratches and dents in the old panels had come there through the passing of thousands of people. He saw his Aunt Augusta standing in front of it, just as he had known her, wearing a flowered apron; and through her back he could see her counting out the flannel underthings which were piled on the left-hand side. He saw himself standing there too, as a little boy, staring at a crack in the wood which had been the shape of a leaping dog, its head downwward. It lasted only a moment, then it was gone.

"Actually, nothing has changed," said the student doubtfully. "It's still the same chest."

The little man shook his head and smiled. "You yourself were different for a moment," he said, "and that is the secret. Shall I go or stay?"

"Go!" said the student. "You are disturbing my peace. I want to be alone and live as I did before. I'm doing well and I want it to stay that way. The old memories upset me. And as far as the thought is concerned—the one I had by the window—that was just a figment of the imagination. Please go away."

But the little man had already gone. The student undressed and got into bed. When he got up next morning he went to a friend and told him what had happened.

"Well done," said the friend, "write it down. Everyone must read it."

The student wrote it down and it came to people's notice, on paper, and people said he was a great scholar. And then he wrote more and it turned into a whole book. The book said that everyone must look after himself, and that, after all, the world was as it was. The people on his side of the street were very proud of him. They came to his room and thanked him for his book.

"It simply had to be said," they said, "and now it has been said."

Then one day the student had studied his fill and he gave a party. The light of the crystal chandelier poured through the windows onto the house opposite and made the panes shine.

But the windows were closed and the curtains drawn and at the front door stood a carriage bearing a small black chest. There was a white cross painted on the lid and the woman standing beside it laid her head on the lid and cried.

"What are you looking at?" asked his friend. "Is something going on?"

But the student turned away and did not answer.

The Last Balloon

O NCE upon a time there was a king who lived in a great palace. He was not very old, but vexation had turned his hair white. For at the entrance to the palace lay a dragon. No one could go in or out, because the dragon had seven heads and every one of its mouths was full of razor-sharp teeth. As soon as anyone rang the front door-bell, he thrust out one of his seven heads and—hoop-la. He ate the visitor and did not even have to swallow twice, he was so huge. In this way he had gobbled up two bakers, a postman and a man who happened to come along and ask if there was anything to be mended.

The king, who loved having visitors, sat at the window and looked out longingly. But the people had more sense than to come. No one came, except his old grandmother, who came because it was the king's birthday. The good soul thought: "I am too tough, the dragon will not eat me up," and she was right. He simply snapped off her head and left the rest lying on the steps.

And the worst thing was that the king began to grow hungry. He put a message into a balloon and blew it up. This was the message:

"PLEASE HELP US. WE CANNOT GO IN OR OUT.
THE KING."

The balloon floated across the country and came down in the courtyard of a castle. Here there lived a famous knight who was known throughout the land for his courage. He read the note and looked up in amazement.

"Strange," he said, "no reward is mentioned."

He had scarcely said the words when a second balloon came floating in. The knight read the second note too and put on his armor at once. He had his horse saddled, and belted on a sword of the finest steel, with

197

which he could cleave through a double wall of bricks. He waited a moment to see if a third balloon was coming and then rode off to consult his old godmother who lived in a little turf hut.

"Dear boy," said the old woman, "what are you up to?"

"Godmother," said the knight, "I cannot turn back now. So give me some good advice."

"Good advice is expensive."

The knight gave her the second letter and when the old woman read it she smiled.

"Well, well, that is worth it," she said, "and so I will help. Here is a bottle of oil. Keep it carefully, for you will not get a second. I have a little mirror for you, too. Do not look in it, but put it in your pocket. And here is a ring. Slip it on her finger and she will be yours. But do not forget your old godmother. I do not live here for fun."

"Old godmother," said the knight, "if all goes well I will not forget you. But alas for you if I fail."

"You will not fail," said the old woman and she watched him lovingly. She was very fond of her godchild, although she was allowed only the crumbs that fell from his table.

The knight rode happily away on his white horse and soon reached the palace. From one of the towers a white hand waved to him, and that was the king's daughter who was shut up there.

"Take heart!" cried the knight, dismounting from his horse and drawing his sword. "I am going to kill the dragon!"

The monster was asleep. No one had come to call for days and so he had fallen into a doze. The knight pulled out a trumpet and played a martial air on it, since he was not given to attacking sleeping beasts. The dragon woke up slowly, and that was a fearful sight. First he opened the eyes on his first head and then on the next, until at last all the eyes in all the heads were open and he was awake. He heaved himself to his feet and growled, but more from surprise than anger. No one had ever ridden to meet him with drawn sword, and that was what the knight was doing. The knight had remounted his horse and was charging straight down upon the dragon.

Swish! Swosh! He cut off the first two heads. Boom! There went the third head, rolling on the ground. But before the knight could raise his sword for a fourth time, the dragon seized his horse in its claws and squeezed it so savagely that its bones cracked. It was a powerful stallion which had carried its master through many perils, but now it fell into a thousand pieces. Each piece moved once and then it was dead.

But the knight had jumped quickly out of the saddle and cut off another three heads before he himself was seized. The dragon had only

one head left, and with that he looked straight into his victim's face. The knight shuddered, for the monster had a squint. The dragon clasped him in its mighty claws but the knight, who was completely encased in steel, did not break. His armor cracked at every joint but it did not give way. Then the monster took the knight in its mouth and ground its razor-sharp teeth. The armor stood up to this treatment, too, although the creaking of the steel could be heard far away. The dragon shook its prey to and fro and suddenly the godmother's little mirror rolled out of an inside pocket of the armor, right under the glittering eyes of the beast. The dragon glanced into the mirror and its reflection scared it to death. As soon as it was dead the king opened the door.

"A thousand thanks, Sir Knight," he said. "I shall not easily forget this. But alas, there is more to do."

"What now?" cried the knight. "Haven't I slain the dragon?"

The king looked embarrassed.

"Didn't you get my third balloon?" he asked.

"No," said the knight, "I saw only two."

The king was confused. "Well," he said, "I am sorry about that, for the most difficult thing was in it."

"What is that, then?" asked the knight.

"I will tell you later," said the king. "First we will take the easiest thing." And he climbed ahead of the knight up a narrow spiral staircase which smelled of pitch and sulphur. When they had climbed it they came into a little room and there sat the princess. In a corner squatted an old woman, warming her hands at the fire.

"As long as that fire burns," said the king, "my daughter cannot get out. It has been burning for nine months and she has not been out all that time. But that will be nothing to you."

"It may well last nine years," said the old woman. "I have time, you know. And just try to put out the flames! You will not succeed."

"But, old woman," said the knight, "why are you doing this?"

"I will tell you," said the witch. "Because she is beautiful and I am ugly. And I want her to be ugly and to be beautiful myself."

"Come now," said the knight, "that surely cannot be."

"Yes, it can!" snarled the old woman, "and the higher the fire burns, the faster it will happen. Look, my hump has already gone and her back is getting more crooked all the time. And take a look at the wrinkles on my face! They are far fewer already, and she is getting more and more of them! And what about my hair! Do you see the fair tresses appearing? Just look at the white streaks in the princess's hair! It is a slow business, but I have time."

She clasped her crooked brown hands together and they were the only thing that had not changed yet. When the knight looked at the princess's hands he saw that they were still white and finely shaped.

"That will come, too," said the old woman, who had followed his glance. "Hands are always the most difficult. If only I had more wood, it would have happened long ago!"

Suddenly the knight thought of the bottle his old godmother had given him. He quickly pulled out the cork and poured the oil on the fire. The flames shot up and roared in the chimney. And the higher the fire burned, the more the princess shrank and the taller grew the old witch. Her wrinkles disappeared like snow in sunshine, her white hair turned to gold and even her crabbed brown hands grew long and slender. Her skin was very white, her mouth cherry red and her eyes shone like two stars in her lovely face.

And in the place where the princess had sat there now sat an old woman, laughing evilly, as if she rejoiced in her own ugliness.

The knight turned to the king. "Look," he said, taking the exquisite girl by the hand, "this is your daughter. For the fire burned so fiercely that her heart too has gone into the other woman. So chase the old woman out of the palace, for she is the witch now and her spell is broken."

So the witch was driven down the stairs and she rolled like a ball down the street. Then she stuck out her little fists, grasped her distaff and blew out of the town like a whirlwind. And along all the streets where she passed the trees shrivelled up, but that was not a bad thing, because new ones were planted next day and the king paid for them out of his own pocket.

And the princess married the knight. At first she hesitated a little, for there was still a bit of the witch left in her and this could be seen from the nails of her left hand, which were a little too long. But when the knight slipped the ring over her finger they fell off of their own accord and the princess threw her arms round his neck and kissed him full on the mouth.

Just at that moment the third balloon, the one with the most difficult task in it, came floating by. The knight grabbed it over the maiden's shoulder, for he wanted to know what its message was, although it had come too late. But when he had read the note he stared at the king in amazement. Then he read it again, for he could not believe his eyes. This was the message:

"P.S. THINK OF YOUR OLD GODMOTHER."

The king smiled.

"To be grateful is the hardest task," he said, "and that is why I kept it to the end."

"But how did you know that I would slay the dragon and drive away the witch?"

"Oh, knights can do those things. But I was not sure if you would also be good to an old woman."

The king was quite right: the knight had completely forgotten his godmother. So now she was invited to eat with them at the palace every Thursday, and every week she came. She peeped over her dish at the young pair and said to anyone who would listen: "*I* did that."

She was right, too, and that was why she was godmother to all their children.

The Three Riddles

ONCE upon a time there was a poor woodcutter. He lived quite alone in the depths of the forest, for he was afraid of nothing and no one. But he was so poor that his shoes were made of oak bark and the laces of willow twigs. His hat was made of grass and when he wanted to smoke a pipe he made one of a hollow chestnut stuffed with dried leaves, and you cannot be poorer than that. But the woodcutter began to weary of his poverty. He went to his godfather, an old wizard who lived in a nearby marsh. He was just studying his book of magic when the woodcutter came in.

"Ah, there is my godson," said the old man. "Are you beginning to weary of being poor?"

"How did you know that?" asked the woodcutter, surprised.

"It's in the book," said the old wizard. "Have a look."

The woodcutter leaned curiously over his godfather's shoulder and this was what he read:

"But the woodcutter began to weary of his poverty. He went to his godfather, an old wizard who lived in a nearby marsh. He was just studying his book of magic when the woodcutter came in."

"You see," said his godfather, "that is how I knew. Everything that is done in the world is in this book. Even what we are talking about now is in it. But if you want to know how to get rich, turn over a page quickly and you will read the future."

In his haste to know, the woodcutter turned over three pages and this is what he read:

"In the very best guest room lived the old wizard, who could do exactly as he pleased. But he did not read his book any more. His eyes had grown weak, and in any case he had known all along that he would be happy. And so he closed the book and was happy."

"It is very nice for me to hear that," said the old man, "but you have gone too far. You can turn only one page."

The woodcutter did so. And this was what he read:

"The woodcutter was so happy that he forgot all about going to bed. He climbed the tree quickly and, sure enough, he saw a dark opening below him, for the tree was hollow."

There was no more, for that was the last line on the page.

"Can I turn over again?" asked the woodcutter eagerly.

"No," said the old wizard. "Then you will be looking too far ahead and that is not good for a man. But because I am your godfather I will help you. The tree is a beech and there is a sign on its bark. I will say no more, for then I would be in trouble. So take courage, my boy, and when you are rich, think of your old godfather."

The woodcutter thanked him heartily and began to walk through the wood. The first evening he counted a hundred beeches, but there was not a mark on any of them. On the second day he counted a thousand beeches, but not one of those had a sign on its bark, either. But on the evening of the third day, just as the sun was setting and he was thinking of going to bed, he saw a huge beech tree standing on a hill top.

"I'll just take a look at that one," thought the woodcutter, "and then I will go to bed."

It was a good thing he did so, for that was the very tree he had been looking for. And in the bark was carved a six. The woodcutter was so happy that he forgot all about going to bed. He climbed the tree quickly and, sure enough, he saw a dark opening below him, for the tree was hollow.

"It is all working out," thought the woodcutter, "and now I will go boldly on."

He dropped down and found himself in a long, dark passage which seemed to have no end. But he stepped out bravely all night, for he was afraid of nothing and no one. Towards daybreak he suddenly saw something bright fluttering ahead of him. It was a big butterfly.

"Where there's a butterfly there's a way out," he said cheerfully, and at that instant he saw a stone staircase leading straight up to the light of day. The good woodcutter was so eager to be rich that he reached the top in three strides and before he knew it he was standing in an open courtyard. The floor was marble and about him he saw the walls of a great castle. Against one of the walls were fifteen heaps of earth and on each of them a name was written in pebbles. And in the shade of an enormous beech tree sat the king on a golden chair.

"Good morning," said the king, "have you come to try?"

"Yes, indeed," said the woodcutter. "What must I do?"

"You must answer three questions," said the king. "And if you get them all right, I will give you my daughter."

"That suits me," said the woodcutter. "Let us begin at once."

"All right," said the king. "Are you afraid?"

"No," said the woodcutter. "I am afraid of nothing and no one. Why do you ask?"

"Because fifteen have tried before you already," said the king, "and they all lie buried there. For you must know: if you do not give the right answers, you will die."

"You are a bright little chap," said the woodcutter, "I am beginning to like you."

The king frowned.

"You are very impertinent," he said. "No one has ever spoken to me like that before. But just wait: soon you will be singing another tune."

Then he led the woodcutter to the council chamber, where all the wise men of the land were already gathered. The king sat down on his throne and gave a sign with his sceptre. At once a trumpet sounded and the king's daughter came in. She really was a lovely girl.

Standing before the woodcutter, she sang:

> "First turn it over
> And then start to add!
> But they were not clever
> And lost all they had."

The woodcutter smiled, for he was thinking of the number on the tree.

"That is a six," he said, "and if you turn it around you have a nine.

And when you add them together, you get fifteen. And those are the fifteen dunces who are buried outside the wall."

The princess blushed scarlet and that showed the woodcutter that he had guessed rightly. The king gazed at him in astonishment. He had never met anything like this before.

"Next question," said the woodcutter.

"This is mine," said the king, "and then we shall see if you are still so cheerful."

He put his crown on his head and sang:

> "If I called it a bird
> I would tell a lie.
> It cannot sing songs
> And yet it can fly.
> It isn't a spider
> And yet it has spun.
> The robe the king wears
> From its thread was won.
> And the riddle I sing
> Is the work of the king!"

The king leaned back in his throne and looked proudly about him, for the riddle really was all his own work. But the woodcutter smiled, remembering the butterfly that had shown him the way.

"If it is not a bird and yet it flies," he said, "then it might be an insect. And if it is not a spider and yet it spins, then it must be a butterfly. And the silken robe you are wearing was woven by it."

The king turned as white as a sheet and gazed speechlessly at the woodcutter. And that showed him that he had guessed rightly.

"Now do I get the princess?" he asked.

"Wouldn't you like to!" cried the king. "But we have only had two questions. Now for the third!"

"No, we have had that already," said the woodcutter. "You asked me outside if I was afraid, and I said no. And it was the right answer, for I am afraid of nothing and no one."

Then the princess clapped her hands and flung her arms round his neck, for she had always wanted a husband who was afraid of nothing and no one. So they married and were given the whole palace to live in.

In the very best guest room lived the old wizard, who could do exactly as he pleased. But he did not read his book any more. His eyes had grown weak, and in any case he had known all along that he would be happy. And so he closed the book and was happy.

The Wily Witch

Designed by Barbara Holdridge
Composed by the Service Composition Company, Baltimore, Maryland
in Baskerville text and display
Printed by the John D. Lucas Printing Company, Inc., Baltimore, Maryland
on 70 lb. Blue White Glatfelter Offset
Bound by The Optic Bindery, Glen Burnie, Maryland
in Kivar Renaissance and Kivar 5 Kidskin